THE LEAGUE OF UNEXCEPTIONAL CHILDREN: GET SMART-ISH

BY GITTY DANESHVARI

ILLUSTRATED BY JAMES LANCETT

LITTLE, BROWN BOOKS FOR YOUNG READERS
www.lbkids.co.uk

LITTLE, BROWN BOOKS FOR YOUNG READERS

First published in the US in 2016 by Little, Brown and Company
First published in Great Britain in 2016 by Hodder and Stoughton

1 3 5 7 9 10 8 6 4 2

Copyright © 2016 by Cat On A Leash, Inc.
Interior art © 2016 by James Lancett

The moral rights of the author and the illustrator have been asserted.

A CIP catalogue record for this book
is available from the British Library.

ISBN 978-0-349-12424-7

Printed and bound by CPI Group (UK) Ltd, Croydon, CR0 4YY

The paper and board used in this book are
made from wood from responsible sources.

MIX
Paper from
responsible sources
FSC
www.fsc.org   FSC® C020471

For Edward John Carlson

THE LEAGUE OF
UNEXCEPTIONAL CHILDREN

CASE FILE: 041315

CASE CLOSED

Following the greatest security breach in American history, twelve-year-olds Jonathan Murray and Shelley Brown were recruited to join the League of Unexceptional Children, a covert network that uses the nation's most average, normal, and utterly forgettable children as spies. Why the average kids? Why not the brainiacs? Or the computer science nerds? Or the jocks?

Well, it's simple: People remember them. But not the unexceptionals. They are the forgotten ones, spending their days reintroducing themselves to kids they've known since preschool. Why? Because they blend in. They live right there in the world's blind spot.

"Is *average* a bad word?"

—Lottie Markman, 11, Ann Arbor, Michigan

CHAPTER 1

OCTOBER 20, 10:28 P.M. EASLETON LABO-
RATORIES. LONDON, ENGLAND

It was a cold night. A foggy night. The kind of night
that makes the hairs on the back of people's necks
prickle, leaving them ill at ease for reasons they can't
quite explain. The city's workers hustled through
London's emptying streets, desperate to find their
way home as soon as possible. And though no one
had any reason to look over their shoulders, they
did. For somewhere deep in the collective unconscious of the city lurked the understanding that

history was about to be made...and not necessarily the good kind.

Standing at the end of a dimly lit alleyway, in front of the doors to Easleton Laboratories, was a thin, scrawny-looking fellow. Clad in a dark green security uniform, the man we would soon come to know as Fred nervously fidgeted with the coins in his pocket.

"What was that?!"

"Oh, come on, Fred, enough with the jitters! You're acting like a schoolgirl about to go on her first date," a paunchy middle-aged man replied.

"Jeffrey, I heard something. I'm sure of it!"

"Mate, there's bugger all here. Well, maybe not bugger all—this is London, so there are probably a few rats and roaches lurking about—"

"I hear someone breathing!" Fred interrupted. "In, out, in, out..."

"That's your own breath, mate," Jeffrey said as he placed a reassuring hand on Fred's shoulder. "Relax! We're guarding a laboratory, not the queen. Our job is pretty simple—stop other nerds from stealing our nerds' work."

"Yeah, you're right," Fred acquiesced unconvincingly. "Nothing scary about nerds...nothing at all."

Located smack-dab in the heart of Central London, Easleton Laboratories was tucked away at the far end of an alley. A lone lamppost sporadically flickered light across the weathered cobblestones. And though cars screeched, buses honked, and people chatted in the distance, Fred and Jeffrey rarely, if ever, saw anyone while on duty.

Click. Clack. Click. Clack.

The sound of shoes grabbed Fred's attention.

"Did you hear that?"

"Of course I heard that," Jeffrey responded as he motioned toward the start of the alley. "It's just some guy from the city—he probably got turned around trying to find the parking lot down the way."

Medium height. Slender. Dressed in a suit, the man appeared to be just who Jeffrey had described: some guy from the city trying to remember where he had parked his car.

Shaking his head back and forth, Fred muttered, "I don't know what's gotten into me lately. Probably all those crime shows I've been watching before bed. Mum always said I was too open to suggestion."

But that wasn't all Fred's mum had said. She also said that his timing was the absolute worst. And boy, was she right. For just as Fred accepted that he was suffering from a terrible case of the nerves and nothing more, danger crept closer. Hidden on the roof of Easleton Laboratories, a shadowy figure watched the unsuspecting duo below. Dressed in a black jumpsuit and a ski mask, the figure had a clear silhouette of a woman. Efficient, precise, and graceful, she unzipped a bag and quickly assembled a tranquilizer gun marked PROPERTY OF THE LONDON ZOO.

"They must be stopped," she stated in a cold, unemotional tone as she loaded a dart, centered the crosshairs on Fred, and fired a horse sedative straight into his bony shoulder.

"Ahhh!" Fred squeaked as his eyes rolled back in his head, his knees buckled, and he slumped to the ground.

"Blimey! It's actually happening! Nerds are attacking!" Jeffrey screamed as he grabbed for the radio on his belt, in a most valiant effort to protect *his* nerds. However, before Jeffrey could even locate the talk button, a dart pierced his right shoulder, instantly knocking him out.

After carefully securing a rope, the masked woman rappelled down the front of the building. Swift and agile, she was standing on the cobblestones less than thirty seconds later. She then pulled out a small mound of red clay and carefully took an imprint of each of the guards' pointer fingers.

"Errgh," Jeffrey gurgled as the woman used a gloved hand to open his mouth and swab the inside of his cheek before turning her attention to Fred.

Mounted on the wall next to the entryway to Easleton Laboratories was a small glass screen where the woman carefully applied the clay impressions, prompting a computerized message to flash IDENTIFICATION VERIFIED as the doors opened into a small vestibule.

Once inside, she slipped the cotton swabs into two cylinder-shaped slots.

"DNA confirmed," a computerized voice announced as the doors to the laboratory opened.

Four minutes and seven seconds passed. The woman emerged from the building, a small glass vial marked LIQ-30 in hand. And just like that, it was out there. A virus so powerful it could *literally*, as in it could actually happen, bring humankind to its knees.

TOP SECRET

"If I had a nickel for every time someone forgot my name, I'd be the first billionaire in history known as 'hey you.'"

—Concha Rey, 12, Madrid, New Mexico

★ SECURE ★
DOCUMENTS

CHAPTER 2

<218968-CR-LOUC-408>

OCTOBER 21, 1:42 A.M. 10 DOWNING STREET.
LONDON, ENGLAND

A worn cotton nightcap hung lopsided over an old woman's face as she charged down the hallway, arms flailing in the air.

"Everyone to the bunker! They're bombing us!"

The woman sang the words over and over again until she reached an imposing wooden door. Her wrinkled, liver-spot-stained hand grabbed hold of the knob and turned it with as much gusto as a ninety-three-year-old woman could muster.

"Everyone to the bunker!" the old woman screamed, jolting the prime minister of the United Kingdom, David Falcon, and his wife from a deep sleep.

"I told you we needed to put a lock on that door," the prime minister's wife moaned as her husband stood up.

"Mrs. Cadogan, the Blitz is over. It ended many, many decades ago."

"Who are you? Where's Prime Minister Churchill?"

"I'm Prime Minister Falcon."

"I don't understand...."

Prime Minister Falcon shook his head and sighed. "Mrs. Cadogan, you have been at Ten Downing Street since 1939. You are nothing short of a national treasure. However, I must tell you that your mind isn't what it used to be. World War Two has been over for quite some time, but as you've aged, your memory seems to have gotten stuck in that period."

"You mean the war's over?" Mrs. Cadogan asked in a faint voice.

"Yes," the prime minister answered.

"Did we win?"

"We're still speaking English, aren't we?" he responded, his patience waning.

"Yes, I suppose we are," Mrs. Cadogan answered before nodding good-bye and wandering back down the hall.

"Poor woman, she spends her nights pacing up and down the corridors," the prime minister's wife uttered as the two returned to bed, eager to fall back asleep. However, before they could even close their eyes, another voice interrupted.

"Excuse me, Prime Minister Falcon, but we have a situation that requires immediate attention."

"What now?" the prime minister grumbled as he grabbed his robe and shoved his feet into a pair of slippers.

Middle-aged with a glass eye, a gangly mess of teeth, and a body that screamed, "I haven't worked out since before the Internet was invented," there was no denying that Randolph Dowager—the source of the interruption—was a rather *unique*-looking man.

"Randolph," the prime minister groaned. "*It* is stuck again."

"My apologies, sir," Randolph replied as he retrieved a mirror from his pocket and adjusted his glass eye. A former operative for MI5 (the United Kingdom's top espionage group), Randolph had lost his eye during a mission. The government regarded it as nothing more than collateral damage—an unintended injury on an unintended target—but to Randolph it was a medal of honor. Albeit one that often found itself stuck looking up at the ceiling.

"My apologies too, sir, for waking you at this most unacceptable hour."

"Yes, yes." The prime minister rushed Randolph along. "Enough with the apologies, on with it!"

"Nina Mitford, an operative in the Bureau of Adolescent Espionage, has gone rogue."

"Honestly, Randolph," the prime minister griped. "BAE agents go missing all the time. They're teenagers, which is to say they're a dreadfully moody bunch of characters. If the wind blows the wrong way, they're ready to break up with the weather!"

"To be clear, sir, Operative Mitford is not missing. She's on the run. At approximately 2300 hours last night, she broke into Easleton Laboratories and stole the vial of LIQ-30."

Prime Minister Falcon stumbled, his legs visibly shaking. "Did you say LIQ-30?"

"I'm afraid I did, sir. BAE and MI5 are scouring the city for Operative Mitford, but have thus far found nary a trace of the girl."

"They're not going to find her," the prime minister stated firmly. "Operative Mitford knows how they think, how they work. Insiders are always the hardest to track. We're going to need help."

"Sir, are you suggesting we bring in an outsider?" Randolph asked.

"Not just an outsider. An American," the prime minister announced as he started down the corridor, a plan taking hold. "Get me the president of the United States."

OCTOBER 22, 7:02 A.M. HEATHROW AIRPORT. LONDON, ENGLAND

"Hey?" twelve-year-old Jonathan Murray called as he exited the plane dressed in his go-to outfit—khaki slacks, a white T-shirt, and sneakers. (He considered this a "respectable look," i.e., one that told the world he planned on being the kind of adult who drove the speed limit and loaded the dishwasher in an orderly fashion.) "Shells? Speak up. I can't hear you," Jonathan continued.

"Way to mess up my flow, Johno," Shelley Brown responded as she pushed back the brim of her fedora. "I was narrating my arrival."

"That's a new one," Jonathan said with a sigh, brushing his flat black locks off his forehead.

Shelley cleared her throat and took on a serious, newscaster-like tone. "Shelley Brown, International Lady of Espionage, arrives in London wearing a gray trench coat, black rain boots, and a felt fedora. Young, attractive, and with a naughty twinkle in her eye, she's ready to take on the world...or maybe just London, since the world is a lot for a twelve-year-old...although she is turning thirteen in eight months, so who knows, maybe she's up for it...."

"You're not a lady," Jonathan corrected Shelley. "You're a *young* lady, which is really just another way of saying kid."

"Ugh," Shelley said, shaking her head. "Always killing my vibe."

"Yup, that's me, professional vibe killer," Jonathan said flatly as he pointed to a yellow customs sign. "It's almost time. What do you say we review our cover?"

"Students attending a Youth in Government conference? Bor-ing, like, I'm asleep already. It's not too late to go with my idea: veterinarians who specialize in canine braces."

"For the last time, we're too young to be veterinarians and no one, I repeat, no one, puts braces on dogs," Jonathan explained. "Our parents bought the youth ambassador story and so will the customs guy."

"I'm not so sure about that. Look at me: I've got *spy* coming out of every pore of my body," Shelley said as she slipped her hands into the pockets of her oversized trench coat.

"And to think I thought that was perspiration," Jonathan deadpanned.

"Are you saying that I sweat a lot? Because if there is one thing Shelley Brown doesn't do, it's sweat a lot. Except when I'm in a sauna or eating at a buffet," Shelley babbled as the customs agent waved the couple in front of them to the podium.

"Passports, please," the agent asked before carefully examining the couple's photographs. "What brings you to the United Kingdom....How long will you be staying....Do you have relatives here....

15

What line of work are you in.... Welcome to London, enjoy your stay.... Next."

And so, Shelley strutted toward the customs agent with the kind of swagger Jonathan had only seen in films. Hips swaying. Shoes tapping. Arms swinging. And though this was an entrance that screamed, "Hey, world, look at me," the man behind the podium barely batted an eyelash. Not even when Shelley removed her fedora, freeing her shoulder-length dirty-blond hair, pushed her round glasses up the bridge of her nose, and whipped out her passport as though flashing a badge. "Shelley Brown here."

"Go on through, kids," the customs agent said after quickly stamping both of their passports.

"But you didn't even look at our pictures! Or ask us any questions!" Shelley blustered as Jonathan pulled her away. "We could be bad guys for all you know! Criminals! Gangsters! Hackers!"

However, the agent didn't hear Shelley. As a matter of fact, *most* people didn't hear Shelley. The girl had the kind of voice that blended with surrounding sounds. So unless someone was extremely close or entirely focused on her, she was almost impossible

to hear. This, of course, only intensified Shelley's
lifelong desire to be noticed.

"Why fight it, Shells?" Jonathan asked as they
walked toward baggage claim. "This is the very reason we were recruited."

"Yeah, I know, but—"

"But nothing," Jonathan interrupted. "You need
to accept the facts. This is our lot in life. Last week
my grandmother sent out her annual family newslet-
ter. Want to know what it said about me? 'Jonathan
Murray is still alive.' It came directly after a para-
graph on my cousin Elena's trip to Peru to build
houses for the poor."

17

"At least she was accurate. You are, in fact, still alive."

"Can you imagine if I died and my own grand-mother didn't notice?"

"Actually, I could totally see that happening. You've got *No one's going to find me until the corpse starts to smell* written all over you," Shelley said before adding, "Unless there are rodents in your house and they eat the body, bones and all. Then no one would know you had died."

"This is exactly the kind of conversation I'd like to avoid when we're with the prime minister," Jonathan stated firmly. "Speaking of which, I think we'd better go straight to Ten Downing Street."

"If they don't have twenty-four-hour room service, I'm going to be seriously upset."

"Shells, Ten Downing Street isn't a hotel. It's the official residence and office for the prime minister of the United Kingdom."

Shelley narrowed her eyes suspiciously. "How do you know that?"

"Everyone knows that," Jonathan replied before quietly adding, "Well, almost everyone..."

"My mom always says, 'Just do your best and I'll be happy,' but when I bring home a C+ she never smiles."

—Rita Reier, 14, Tarzana, California

CHAPTER 3

<112159-RR-LOUC-348>

OCTOBER 22, 9:32 A.M. 10 DOWNING STREET.
LONDON, ENGLAND

The man was thin and wiry. He wore a pristinely tailored navy suit and an expensive yet understated wristwatch. Stuck in a perpetual state of scowling, Prime Minister Falcon was exactly what Jonathan and Shelley expected of a government official— serious and imposing.

"President Arons informs me that you are the team responsible for recently stopping the sale of classified government information, as well as bringing the vice president's kidnapper to justice," Prime Minister Falcon said in a stiff and formal manner befitting a conversation with the queen.

"To you he may be the vice president, but to me he's just Carl, a close personal friend," Shelley stated proudly while seated before the prime minister's desk.

"In the spirit of full disclosure, I feel you should know that Shelley has an incredibly low bar for what constitutes a friend," Jonathan chimed in. "If you so much as wave at her, she'll consider you a bestie."

"But am I correct in assuming that you two were responsible for the success of the aforementioned mission?" Prime Minister Falcon pressed on.

"You are, sir," Jonathan confirmed, and then quickly bit his tongue to stop himself from adding, *"But I'm pretty sure the whole thing was a fluke."*

"Good," the prime minister responded with a nod. "I do not ask for foreign aid easily. Only the most grave and dangerous of situations has brought me to do so today."

"PM—may I call you PM?"

"Please don't," Jonathan whispered to Shelley.

"You needn't worry," Shelley went on, "because while my middle name isn't 'Grave and Dangerous,' it would be if it weren't illegal for minors to change their names without parental permission."

Prime Minister Falcon's stiff expression grew strained as he looked from Shelley to Jonathan expectantly.

"Oh, me? I don't have a middle name, which is actually a good thing when you hear the ones my parents were considering...Flash, Boon, River...I mean, what were they thinking? I could never pull off any of those names."

"No way. Frank or Larry, maybe," Shelley added.

"I do not wish to offend you two, but—" the prime minister began.

Shelley held up her left hand. "Don't worry, it takes a lot to offend us, right, Johno?"

"Right. It's actually one of our strongest assets."

"You two seem terribly inept, rather shockingly so," Prime Minister Falcon declared unapologetically.

"Inept? You mean like we don't know what we're doing?" Shelley asked.

"Exactly," the prime minister answered.

"That's because we don't know what we're doing. And we're pretty much not good at anything," Jonathan explained.

"I hate to disagree with my partner, but I actually have quite a few hidden talents."

"She doesn't," Jonathan stated emphatically. "But what we do have is an ability to blend in, to go through life without registering on anyone's radar. Why? Because we're average, forgettable, normal. In the words of the League's chief operating agent, Hammett Humphries, we live in the world's blind spot."

"And that blind spot gives us access to just about everything," Shelley said as she removed her glasses and looked the prime minister straight in the eye. "You may not believe it now, but in the end, you'll wish all your spies were as unexceptional as we are."

"This is a most interesting theory. It is not the talent of the operative that matters, but the operative's ability to go unnoticed," the prime minister pondered quietly.

"We saved our government from some pretty scary stuff, and if you'll let us, we'll do our best to help you too," Jonathan said.

The prime minister stared at the boy for a few seconds before turning to Randolph and nodding.

"Two nights ago a BAE agent—that's the Bureau of Adolescent Espionage—named Nina Mitford went AWOL," Randolph said while placing a photo of the teenage girl on the table in front of Jonathan and Shelley. "She disconnected her tracking device, turned off her cell phone, and then broke into a laboratory that handles low-security experiments... with one very important exception."

"Ooooh," Shelley said, leaning in, "I'm sensing this is about to get good."

"To fully understand this story, I must first tell you about the chiropterologist," Randolph began before pausing. "That is someone who studies bats."

"No need to state the obvious, Randolph," Shelley interjected while Jonathan rolled his eyes.

"The chiropterologist, Dr. Kashef, was well known in the research community for a variety of reasons, one of which was that he was a certified genius with an IQ of one sixty. However, a few months ago, while on a research trip in Africa, he was bitten by a previously unknown mutation of the common fruit bat. Within weeks he was a changed man—easily distracted, confused, unable to focus for more than a few seconds at a time and, as such, less intelligent—by thirty IQ points, to be exact. You see, this mutated group of bats carried a virus that attacks the brain's frontal lobe, permanently affecting a person's ability to focus and therefore their intelligence. The virus spreads via saliva. And though this small colony of bats was destroyed, one vial of the virus was brought back to the United Kingdom for research."

"Dr. Kashef kissed a bat, didn't he? Listen, I'm not judging; weird things happen in the dark. Once during a blackout, I let my sister's hamsters out of the cage, only to hunt them down like a lion would rabbits....I turned into a real animal...until the lights came on. Then I went back to watching reality TV," Shelley said, prompting the prime minister to whisper to Randolph, "It is not just the loss of great minds that scares me, but what will happen to those already lacking."

Randolph nodded as a creaking sound began to emanate from the closet to the left of the prime minister's desk. The faint noise morphed into a raucous shuffling, prompting all in the room to turn.

"Don't tell me we have another rodent infestation," the prime minister remarked as the door flung open, revealing a tall man in a double-breasted gray pin-striped suit, with a well-oiled head of black hair.

"Randolph, call security!" Prime Minister Falcon shrieked as he pushed his chair away from the desk.

"Hammett!" Shelley and Jonathan cried in unison as the man popped a toothpick into his mouth and sauntered into the room.

"No need for security, Prime Minister," Hammett said as he approached the desk, right hand

extended. "The name's Hammett, with two *t*'s, Hammett Humphries."

"The chief operating agent for the League of Unexceptional Children?" the prime minister asked.

"That's me, live and in the flesh," Hammett said as he pulled the toothpick from his mouth.

"Yes, but what on earth were you doing in my closet?" Prime Minister Falcon demanded as he banged his fist against the desk.

"You're a feisty one, aren't you?" Hammett said with a sly smile. "Let me give it to you short and simple. These two here, they might not look like much, or talk like much, or even know much, but they're going to save you, I guarantee it. However, unexceptionals are like porcupines in a cage full of gorillas. They need special handling, so President Arons thought it best I was on the ground in London, just in case."

"Very well, we can accept that your spies need a chaperone, but that still doesn't explain what you were doing in the closet," Randolph snapped brusquely.

"What can I say? I like to make an entrance," Hammett said just as a red-haired woman dressed in a traditional white nurse's uniform exited the closet.

"The Thames flood of 1928 killed fourteen people. Gray and bloated; that's how the bodies looked when they pulled them from the river," the stern-faced woman announced to the room.

"Who in the bloody heck is this?" Prime Minister Falcon griped, clearly frustrated by the stream of visitors in his office.

"This here's my colleague Nurse Maidenkirk. She's a great broad, but she never has anything cheerful to say; it's just one horror story after another," Hammett explained.

"Charming lot, you Americans," the prime minister grumbled sarcastically as he eyed the motley crew. "Now, unless there are any other people hiding in the closet, may we please get back to the rather pressing matter at hand?!"

Randolph nodded and quickly resumed his briefing. "After interviewing Operative Mitford's friends and colleagues at BAE, we've learned that she is a passionate environmentalist. One who has grown increasingly disillusioned by our government's failure to support legislation that would protect England's nature preserves. And with an initiative to allow oil drilling in protected areas coming before Parliament next week, we believe she plans on using LIQ-30 on select ministers to sway the vote in her favor."

"For as you can imagine, the more confused a person is, the easier he or she is to manipulate," the prime minister added.

"Trust me, I know," Shelley said, motioning toward Jonathan. "I've seen this one manipulated by squirrels in the park; they worked him over for every last piece of popcorn he had. It was pathetic."

"Once LIQ-30 is out there, there's no stopping it. It will be a plague more destructive than any we've ever known: a plague of dimming intelligence," Prime Minister Falcon continued, completely ignoring Shelley's comments.

"Not to worry, PM, we're on it like white on rice or brown on rice, depending on what kind of rice you prefer to eat," Shelley babbled, then extended her arms. "What do you say we seal the deal with a hug?"

"I don't think so," Prime Minister Falcon responded coldly.

"Hugs have helped many a world leader deal

with the pain of childhood. A few seconds in these bad boys and you forget all about the time your parents left you at the rest stop in Yellowstone."

"And on that very uncomfortable note, I think we're done," Jonathan announced as he pulled Shelley away from the prime minister.

"On that we agree," Randolph said. "Mr. Humphries, Nurse Maidenkirk, as the operatives will be at BAE headquarters this afternoon, I do not believe we will be needing your services any further today."

"Is that your polite way of saying we don't have clearance?" Hammett asked as he popped a new toothpick into his mouth. "Not to worry, we can take a hint. Can't we, Maidenkirk?"

"There was a dead bird near the gate," Nurse Maidenkirk said, eyes twinkling with excitement. "It probably flew into a window and broke its neck. I think we ought to have it stuffed by a local taxidermist as a souvenir from the trip."

"I feel it my duty to tell you that this woman isn't an actual nurse, so don't let her give you any shots, okay?" Jonathan whispered to Randolph.

TOP SECRET

"Everyone says I take the easy
way out, but if that's true, why
am I having such a hard time?"

—Stella Klewans-Duboz, 14, New Orleans,
Louisiana

CHAPTER 4

<547852-SK-LOUC-227>

OCTOBER 22, 11:03 A.M. BAE HEADQUARTERS. LONDON, ENGLAND

Barren. Cold. High-tech. These were Jonathan's and Shelley's first impressions of the lobby of the Bureau of Adolescent Espionage.

"Operatives 2397 and 2398 reporting for duty," Randolph said to one of the many guards standing at attention.

"Follow me," a gruff-looking man barked, and then led Jonathan and Shelley to two large metal-and-glass boxes in the corner of the room.

"Step inside. We're scanning for tracking devices and bugs, as well as logging your features for our facial recognition software. At BAE we do not believe in identification cards, as there is always a chance that they can be counterfeited. A face, however, cannot."

"Talk about high-tech," Jonathan mumbled as the two stepped inside the boxes.

"Sure beats climbing through a fridge of pork products," Shelley said, thinking of the League of Unexceptional Children's headquarters hidden behind Famous Randy's Hot Dog Palace.

Following the scans, Randolph led Jonathan and Shelley to a door marked SOUTH CORRIDOR while explaining, "Rogue operatives are dreadful for office morale, so we thought it best to set up our central command away from the others. After all, we needn't flaunt Operative Mitford's betrayal."

"Maybe it's just me, but traitors actually lift my spirits; they make me feel better about myself. Like, it suddenly doesn't seem so bad that I cheated off Stefan Lindeman in math class and still managed to fail the test," Shelley rambled as Jonathan smiled, relieved that Randolph couldn't hear her soft voice over the white noise pumping through the halls (a security measure to stop operatives from eavesdropping).

"It's basic, but it will have to do," Randolph stated as he opened the door to a stale, windowless room at the end of the corridor with wall-to-wall gray carpeting, a couple of desks, and a map of London.

"So it's just Shelley and me working the case?" Jonathan asked as he looked around the empty room. "Are you sure that's a good idea?"

Shelley cleared her throat and then grabbed hold of Randolph's arm to make sure he was listening. "Please ignore my partner. Acting insecure is part of his cover."

Jonathan sighed and thought, *If only that were true.*

"You needn't worry. The others are on their way," Randolph responded to Jonathan. "Now, in regards to your backstories, President Arons has requested that no additional BAE operatives, outside of Vera and Felix, whom you worked with in America, be told of your true identity as members of the League of Unexceptional Children. So we have told the team that you are spies from America—no more, no less."

"Got it. Now, what kind of gadgets are you tricking us out with? Because I should tell you, I'm kind of a tech whiz," Shelley bragged as Jonathan shook his head.

"After reading your files, we have decided it best to limit your exposure to technology. To be honest, we weren't even sure we were going to give you cell phones at first," Randolph explained as he motioned for the two to take seats.

"I'm reading between the vines here, but it was because of our accents, wasn't it? You didn't want to be forced to listen to a couple of Americans on the phone."

"Shells, it's reading between the *lines*, not the vines," Jonathan clarified.

"No, it's *vines*, as in it's hard to read something covered in vines," Shelley explained.

"I'm afraid Jonathan is right on this one. And I can assure you the issue was not your accents, but rather your track records," Randolph stated as he pulled up a file on his iPad. "It appears that you, Shelley, have lost a total of eighteen phones, twelve of which were landlines—as in phones that plug into the wall."

"You know, I want to say you're wrong. But something about this sounds vaguely familiar," Shelley acknowledged.

"And as for you, Jonathan. You have only destroyed two phones in your life. But both times resulted in fire. I believe the first incident involved you sticking a slice of bread in your pocket and your phone in the toaster—"

"And the second a frozen burrito in my back-pack and my phone in the microwave," Jonathan interrupted.

"So it was nothing short of a miracle that I was able to convince the powers that be to trust both of you with mobiles," Randolph said as the sound of a door opening distracted Jonathan and Shelley.

Confident, striking, and exceptional—these were Shelley's first impressions of the trio of operatives entering the room. Everything from the manner in which they walked, dressed, and stood silently com-municated that they were nothing short of espionage royalty. The faint voice in the back of Shelley's mind, the one she always tried her best to ignore, suddenly erupted. *These kids know what they're doing! Run! Get out as fast as you can! They're going to see straight through you!*

But just as Shelley prepared to dart from the room without so much as an explanation, another voice appeared. Only this one played fast and loose with the truth, thereby tricking Shelley into feeling important, strong, and confident. A surge of adrenaline whipped through her body as she listened to the voice list her many "talents." *Best puppy cuddler in the United States, sampler of Korean food, break-dancer, air guitar master, snoreless sleeper...*

"Where are Vera and Felix?" Jonathan asked as he looked over the unfamiliar faces.

"Unfortunately, they had to take a slight detour to rural Mongolia. They're our only operatives fluent in the Khalkha dialect, so we had no choice but to send them," Randolph said.

"What a shame! I was really looking forward to seeing good old *Ver* and *Fel* again," Shelley said, turning to the three operatives. "We had some crazy times with them last week. Wait until you guys hear about it—"

"Shells, it was a top secret mission, which means

we can never, ever talk about it," Jonathan stated, raising his eyebrows in an effort to drive the point home.

"Um, I know, Johno," Shelley covered poorly. "If you had let me finish, I was going to say, *'Wait until you guys hear about it…when we're all dead… because when we're ghosts, security breaches no longer matter.'*"

"Since your deaths are most likely some ways off—although in this line of work you never know— may I suggest we get on with the introductions,"

Randolph said, and then pointed to a petite redheaded girl in a blue-and-yellow plaid dress. "Jonathan, Shelley, may I present Hattie Fleming."

"Good afternoon, young lady and young gentleman, I am most pleased to make your acquaintance," the girl offered in a staid, formal tone of voice. "As you will soon learn, I am something of an anomaly— a technology expert who prefers the simpler things in life, such as a fine cucumber sandwich or a weekend shooting clay pigeons."

"As a recent convert to vegetarianism, I am staunchly anti–pigeon assassins," Shelley declared, narrowing her eyes at Hattie.

"How recent was the conversion? You ate a sausage-and-egg sandwich with a side of bacon for breakfast," Jonathan reminded Shelley.

"Darn it! Every time I'm hungry I forget I'm a vegetarian," Shelley lamented, and then pursed her lips. "In light of what I just heard, I think it's best I retract the pigeon assassin comment...so please consider it retracted...like it never happened...even though it did...but now let's all pretend that it didn't."

"They're *clay* pigeons, not actual birds. You do understand the difference, don't you?" Hattie asked.

"Yet another reason I'm glad I retracted my previous statement, *non*–pigeon killer," Shelley said. "And just so you know, Jonathan hates cucumber sandwiches."

"She grows on you," Jonathan added quietly. "Sort of like mold on a piece of fruit."

After a few seconds of awkward stares, Randolph pointed to a boy dressed in a beige corduroy suit, with dark brown skin and black curly locks that added an extra inch to the circumference of his head. "This young man is Oliver Lakeshore, although he prefers to be called Oli."

The boy nodded hello to Jonathan and Shelley before clearing his throat. "I am a historian, which is quite useful in our field because, in the words of philosopher George Santayana, 'Those who cannot remember the past are condemned to repeat it.'"

"And those who quote other people are condemned to bore all those around them," an extremely tall and muscular blond boy at the end of the line huffed. "I mean, what kind of spy is a historian? It's utterly ludicrous!"

"The prime minister doesn't think so," Oli answered loudly.

"And this is our biochemical expert, Darwin Chapman. Equal parts intelligence and nuisance," Randolph interjected.

"Come on, Teeth, I'm not that bad," Darwin said with a wry smile.

"Do not call me Teeth!" Randolph snapped.

"And you thought it was bad when I called the prime minister PM," Shelley whispered to Jonathan.

"Oh, come on, don't get your knickers in a twist. It's not like I'm calling you Eye or anything," Darwin continued.

"People of my generation did not get braces. It simply was not done," Randolph stated impatiently.

"So what are your specialties?" Darwin asked Jonathan and Shelley as he stepped forward, towering over the two.

"Mahjong," Shelley exclaimed without thinking. "And backgammon," she said, pointing at Jonathan.

Darwin shook his head and laughed. "You two are experts in old people's games? Why on earth would we need you to help us track Nina?"

"Dar? Can I call you Dar? Or would you prefer Win?" Shelley asked.

"I would prefer *Darwin*, as that is my name."

"It appears there's a lot you don't know about Nina, because she was in fact a very dedicated and highly gifted mahjong-ist and backgammon-ist."

"And environmentalist," Jonathan said while pinching Shelley in an attempt to stop her improvising.

"Now then," Randolph spoke up, "if we are finished with introductions, I would like an update on Operative Mitford."

Hattie raised her left hand, cloaked in a pristine white glove, to indicate that she was prepared to speak first. "Such an odd bird, that Nina. She used the name of her neighbor's pet rabbit as the password for her e-mail, and we all know she doesn't even like rabbits. Not that she needed a difficult password; there's nothing to protect. The whole account has been wiped clean except for a few e-mails from her grandmother requesting cakes from a local bakery," Hattie finished with a huff. "Shameful, isn't it? A grandmother who doesn't bake."

Sensing that Hattie might be tempted to continue her condemnation of Nina's grandmother,

Randolph spoke up. "And Operative Mitford's room at boarding school?"

"A dead end. No explosives residue. No interesting gadgets. Just a few ferns and a couple of pictures," Darwin answered.

"And her cell phone?" Randolph continued.

"Turned off," Oli jumped in, clearly eager to take part in the briefing.

"We've installed facial recognition software at Heathrow, Gatwick, and City airports on the off chance she tries to flee the country on a fake passport," Hattie said.

"So what do we do now?" Jonathan asked.

"We wait," Randolph answered.

"In the words of William Faulkner, 'And sure enough even waiting will end...if you can just wait long enough,'" Oli stated with dramatic flair.

"Forget the waiting—the real question is, will the quotes ever end?" Darwin grumbled.

"I must admit they are a bit tiresome, Oli," Hattie offered quietly.

"You mean like your stories about making blood sausage and Yorkshire pudding aren't?" Oli hit back.

"Dear boy, you clearly do not understand that blood sausage and Yorkshire pudding are an important part of the British culture! What's next, an attack on tea?"

"If this is how they treat each other," Jonathan whispered to Shelley, "what are they going to do to us?"

"Sometimes I wonder what other people think of me, but then I remember they don't."

—Tag Heren, 9, Montgomery, Alabama

CHAPTER 5

<755822-TH-LOUC-183>

OCTOBER 22, 4:07 P.M. CLARIDGE'S HOTEL.
LONDON, ENGLAND

"Lovely, isn't it?" Hattie said as the five young spies walked into the foyer of London's famous Claridge's hotel. "A most impressive establishment. They've been serving afternoon tea here for over a century."

"During the Second World War, the kings of Norway, Greece, and Yugoslavia stayed here. As a matter of fact, Prime Minister Winston Churchill went so far as to designate room two-twelve Yugoslavian domain so that Crown Prince Alexander the Second could be born in his own country," Oli recounted as Darwin feigned snoring.

"Sorry," Darwin said as he placed his hand on Oli's shoulder, "but the only thing more tiresome than your love of historical trivia is Hattie's obsession with the difference between clotted cream and whipped cream."

"An Englishman who does not know the difference between clotted cream and whipped cream is not an Englishman," Hattie stated decisively before motioning toward the other side of the room. "I've booked the corner table so that we may have a bit of privacy."

"So this is how BAE operatives roll," Shelley said as they arrived at the elegant table, complete with well-polished silver and hand-painted plates. "I could get used to this."

"As this is your first trip to London, we thought you might enjoy seeing a few of the sights," Darwin said as a selection of crust-free sandwiches, scones, jams, and clotted cream arrived on a tiered serving tray.

"Thank you," Jonathan said, unsure what to make of the trio of operatives, who, in a very short period of time, had shown both their flair for insulting one another, as well as minding their manners.

"I can't lie—" Shelley began.

"And yet you do it so often," Jonathan mumbled.

"I'm a little disappointed there isn't any carrot cake. It's our favorite," Shelley said.

"Strange that you should mention carrot cake; Nina absolutely loved it. Last year she even brought one into headquarters to celebrate her birthday," Darwin added, and then looked to Hattie for confirmation.

"A most delicious cake. Very moist," Hattie responded.

"So you guys knew Nina well?" Jonathan inquired seconds before shoving the remaining half of a sandwich into his mouth.

"We were all recruited within months of one another. We trained together. We struggled through our first assignments together," Darwin answered before turning to Oli. "How long has it been now?"

"Almost three years."

"And you didn't see this coming?" Shelley asked while silently rejoicing in the fact that these prodigies, these espionage exceptionals, had clearly missed all the signs.

"'When people talk, listen completely. Most people never listen.' Ernest Hemingway. Which is to say, perhaps we weren't listening as closely to what she was saying as we should have been," Oli admitted.

"The poor thing. She set out to change the world, and in the end it was the world that changed her," Hattie said as Darwin signaled the waiter to bring the check.

"If you have time, there are a few places we'd like to show you," Darwin said to Jonathan and Shelley. "We think they might help you understand where Nina went wrong."

On a narrow one-way street lined with small
mews houses painted a flurry of colors from pale
pink to sky blue, Darwin stopped and motioned for
Jonathan and Shelley to come closer.

"I know the Easter Bunny isn't real..." Shelley
whispered to Jonathan.

"You're talking about the Easter Bunny?" Jonathan asked, shaking his head at the randomness of
the topic.

"But if he was real, and he lived in London, he
would totally live here," Shelley said, motioning
toward the candy-colored homes.

"Closer," Darwin insisted, pulling Jonathan and
Shelley so close that they were momentarily distracted by the boy's perfectly straight, glossy white
teeth. "Nina, like the rest of us, grew frustrated
standing on the sidelines watching crimes happen.
Why? Because the police, Scotland Yard, BAE—
we don't have the power to stop people before they
commit the crime, not without a mountain of proof.
So instead we wait for it all to go wrong just so we
can step in and try to fix it."

51

"Take number forty-four for instance," Oli said as he pulled at the sleeves of his corduroy jacket. "A man named Victor Welsh used to live here. Divorced and going through a bitter custody dispute, his wife called the police five times warning that he was planning to kidnap their child, but the police couldn't do anything about it, as they lacked concrete evidence. Two days after the mother's last call to the authorities, Victor disappeared with their daughter. And seven months later, we still haven't a clue where the man is."

"Such a dreadful, horrid fellow," Hattie remarked as she pulled a crumpled tissue from the sleeve of her dress and dabbed her eyes. "I should like to see him squeezed through a meat grinder for what he's done to that poor woman and her child."

Jonathan stared at Hattie, brow furrowed. "I don't understand." It was a sentiment he had expressed countless times in his life and yet somehow, at this moment, it felt different. The weight of the story pressed down on him. "How could you just stand by and let someone kidnap a child?"

"It's the law. You cannot arrest someone based on a hunch or gut feeling. You need actual proof," Oli explained.

"This next one was a personal favorite of Nina's," Darwin announced as he turned the corner, entering a well-manicured square. "The CEO of Felton Oil lives here. One of England's richest men. And for a good reason. He's a notorious miser, willing to push everything to the limit just to save a penny."

"A most wicked man!" Hattie snapped. "He wiped out entire ecosystems. And all because he thought that faulty old oil tanker could make one last run. But of course it couldn't. And the next thing you know, Mr. Felton was on television, apologizing for the terrible *accident* that had taken place. An accident? Hardly! Anyone with half a brain knew that tanker had less than a twenty percent chance of crossing the Atlantic without a spill."

"As it turns out, a heavy burden of proof is not just the innocent man's friend, but the criminal's as well," Oli added.

"We do not agree with Nina's tactics, but we understand her frustration," Darwin explained. "After all, the bad guys do appear to be winning more and more these days."

"Maybe Nina has a point; maybe someone should take the law into their own hands," Shelley mused aloud, prompting Oli, Darwin, and Hattie to exchange quick glances.

"Is that what you believe?" Darwin asked Shelley. "That the end justifies the means?"

"No, I don't think so," Shelley finally answered. "If everyone took the law into their own hands, the world would go crazy."

Darwin nodded and smiled faintly. "Good to hear. For a second there, I thought we might have another Nina on our hands."

It was only because Shelley was standing so close to Darwin (a requirement for being heard) that she noticed the boy's smile didn't quite reach his eyes. There was something unconvincing about his reaction, something that nagged at Shelley. However, before she could figure out what it might mean, Oli jumped in.

"As you have most likely ascertained by now, we know Nina very well, which means we are going to catch her, and we are going to stop her," Oli stated confidently.

"But we prefer to work alone," Darwin interjected bluntly. "Please know it's nothing personal."

It sure feels personal, Jonathan thought. How

was it possible that they were being rejected as spies before they even had a chance to start?

"Plus, there are so many splendid sights to see in London—Big Ben, Parliament, the National Gallery—why waste your trip working? We can easily cover for you two with Randolph," Hattie added.

Shelley ripped off her glasses and shook her head. "Not a chance! Once we've been assigned a mission, nothing can stop us. Except for a tsunami or falling into a coma or being thrown in prison or—"

"There's something off about you two," Darwin interrupted. "I can't quite put my finger on it, but you're not like any other operatives we know."

Jonathan and Shelley stared blankly at Darwin as they silently reviewed their options. Telling the truth was off the table, as President Arons had explicitly instructed them not to speak of the League of Unexceptional Children. However, hiding their incompetence and lack of training was near impossible.

"Interesting," Shelley stalled, rubbing her chin. "We're not like other operatives? How so?"

"The two of you have an air about you, an air of inability. Dare I say, you seem to be the Neville

Chamberlains of espionage," Oli declared, and then broke into a fit of laughter along with Darwin and Hattie.

Eager as ever to fit in, Shelley joined the raucous laughter. However, the second she did, the trio abruptly stopped.

Oli leaned in, mere inches from Shelley's smudged glasses, and asked, "Am I to take it that you actually *know* who Neville Chamberlain is?"

Shelley rolled her eyes at Oli and confidently replied, "Shelley Brown knows all about Neville Chamberlain."

Brow furrowed, sweat pooling along his upper lip, Jonathan did the only thing he could think of—he sighed loudly.

"Go on, then," Darwin prompted Shelley. "Tell us about Mr. Chamberlain."

Again, the voice of doubt in Shelley's head appeared. *Run! Get out! They know you're nothing but a fraud!*

Don't you dare run! You can do this! You're nothing short of a genius on your feet, Shelley's voice of confidence countered.

After banging her palm against her forehead,

Shelley broke into a goofy smile. "Wait, when I said Shelley Brown, you thought I was talking about myself? I can see how that could have been confusing, but I was actually talking about my fourth-grade history teacher. She just so happens to also be called Shelley Brown. What can I say? It's a popular name."

"I'm afraid I don't follow. If you were not in fact referring to yourself when you said 'Shelley Brown knows all about Neville Chamberlain,' then why were you laughing?" Hattie inquired.

"Quite the detective, aren't you?" Shelley offered through a tense smile.

"Dear girl, have you forgotten that I'm an operative?" Hattie replied.

"My mother always said that if my brain were a cheese, it would be Swiss, because of all the holes in my memory," Shelley rambled awkwardly, all the while searching her mind for some way, any way, to bring this conversation to an end.

"You still haven't explained why you were laughing," Darwin interjected.

"That's what's known as...a future laugh. As in, I'm laughing now so that in the future when I understand the joke, I don't need to waste any time actually laughing," Shelley explained.

"Future laughs are very popular in the United States," Jonathan lied, and then whispered to Shelley, "I'm pretty sure Neville Chamberlain's a character in Harry Potter."

"That's Neville Longbottom! Even I know that," Shelley whispered back.

"Neville Chamberlain was Britain's most ineffective and inept prime minister. He was the man who famously supported appeasement with Hitler before the start of the Second World War," Oli explained.

"You have heard of Hitler, haven't you?" Darwin asked with his trademark sly smile.

"Yes!" Jonathan and Shelley answered in unison.

"Good. For a second there I was starting to wonder whether Glasses and Khaki were duds in the brains department," Darwin responded. "Because we don't work with duds."

"Neither do we," Shelley retorted.

"And you're quite certain that you're up for the mission?" Oli inquired.

"I'd say we're more like *sort of* certain," Jonathan answered.

"Very well, then. No time to waste. We'd best start back toward Downing Street—it's a bit of a walk from here," Hattie said as she led the charge down the street.

OCTOBER 22, 6:03 P.M. STREET. LONDON, ENGLAND

"You see, it was a Sunday in mid-November, which is, of course, prime partridge season," Hattie explained to Jonathan as the two walked side by side, the others trailing behind them.

"I'm sorry, what season?" Jonathan asked.

"Partridge season. Don't tell me you've never heard of partridge season?"

"Unfortunately, I'm only familiar with the basics—summer, fall, winter, and spring," Jonathan answered honestly.

"Partridge season, not to be confused with pheasant or grouse season, is September first to February first," Hattie continued.

"Excuse me, but may I interrupt?" Oli said, approaching from behind.

"Yes, of course!" Jonathan answered a little too enthusiastically.

"Hattie, you simply must hear what Shelley just said," Oli shrieked, barely controlling his laughter.

"I don't know what the big deal is. 'Life's in the meat tails' is a pretty common saying," Shelley said with a shrug.

"Life's in the *details*," Jonathan corrected Shelley.

"No, it's *meat tails*. As in life is full of surprises, like finding really good meat on an animal's tail," Shelley said, and then stopped to rub her chin. "On second thought, maybe it is *details*?"

"Will she ever learn?" Jonathan wondered aloud as the group approached the heavily guarded gate in front of 10 Downing Street.

"We do hope you both sleep well, safe and sound in your beds," Hattie said to Jonathan and Shelley, waving good night.

"*Safe?*" Darwin asked. "Is an operative ever really safe?"

"Not until they're dead," Oli answered, as the trio walked into the night.

"It's not that I'm forgettable, I'm just not memorable."

—Louie Avila, 9, Seattle, Washington

CHAPTER 6

<886486-LA-LOUC-786>

OCTOBER 23, 2:06 A.M. RIVER THAMES. LONDON, ENGLAND

It was a most unusual sight. A speedboat carrying five kids, cutting through the river Thames at just past two in the morning. Seated on a bench at the back of the boat were Jonathan and Shelley, huddled together, the wind chilling them to the bone. Seemingly unaffected by the briskness, Oli and Hattie flanked Darwin as he moored the boat in front of the Tower of London, a royal fortress that had been used as everything from a mint to an armory to a prison and torture chamber, and much more.

"As we said earlier, Nina turned on her cell phone for less than six seconds tonight," Darwin explained as they disembarked from the boat.

"But six seconds was all I needed to track her signal," Hattie said, pulling a tissue from her sleeve. "What a terrible pest the cold is for my sinuses!"

Oli stood staring at the Tower of London, index finger tapping his temple. "It makes perfect sense, now that I think about it. For just last week I saw Nina reading a book on Anne Boleyn." He then turned to Jonathan and Shelley. "You know who Anne Boleyn is, don't you?"

"So this is going to be a thing now? Asking us who everyone is," Jonathan grumbled. "Great."

Annoyed by the smirk on Darwin's face, an over-whelming desire to prove the smug boy wrong took hold of Shelley. "As a matter of fact, we're friends on Facebook."

"You're friends with Anne Boleyn on Face-book?" Darwin repeated, breaking into uncon-trolled laughter.

Shelley's face contorted as her cheeks burned

with embarrassment. "Okay, fine. We're not friends on Facebook. I'm going to need to retract that whole statement."

"Dear girl, another retraction?" Hattie noted, shaking her head.

"Trust me, it's easier to nod and accept than to question," Jonathan offered before releasing an epically long sigh.

"Nod and accept that your partner claimed to be Facebook friends with Henry the Eighth's wife Anne Boleyn? I don't think so," Darwin replied haughtily.

"Henry the Eighth was the king of England from 1509 to 1547. He's rather notorious for having six wives, two of whom he had executed, Anne Boleyn being one of them. And it just so happens that she was tried and executed here at the Tower of London," Oli explained. "Don't they teach history in the United States?"

Jonathan and Shelley stared at Oli, as they did any time they were unsure of what to do next.

"Of course they teach us history," Jonathan finally responded. "They just prefer to focus on the United States."

"Exactly!" Shelley concurred. "We're just really into ourselves, so we don't have time to study your dead kings and their wives."

"I do loathe to interrupt this history lesson, but it's been just over an hour since I picked up Nina's cell signal," Hattie said urgently. "We must move quickly or we're liable to lose her."

OCTOBER 23, 2:18 A.M. TOWER OF LONDON. LONDON, ENGLAND

Standing in front of one of the many service entrances to the Tower of London, Hattie, Darwin, and Oli carefully assessed the situation by scanning the area with infrared binoculars and checking for radio signals on their phones.

"We're coming up clean. There aren't any guards close by, making this as good a moment as any to break in," Darwin announced to the group.

"Break in? Don't we have permission to be here?" Jonathan asked.

"Permission really slows us down. We don't see the point," Darwin answered casually.

"Why am I always winding up in situations like this?" Jonathan mumbled under his breath.

"Because you're a spy," Shelley answered firmly as she grabbed hold of Jonathan's arm.

"Right," Jonathan reminded himself. "I'm a spy."

"Hattie, we need the code," Darwin said as he pointed to the number pad attached to the door's lock.

"So it appears," Hattie said as she removed her gloves, headband, and clip-on earrings before pulling out her cell phone and typing in nearly one hundred different numbers.

"Amazing, isn't it?" Oli whispered to Jonathan and Shelley. "All she talks about is clotted cream

and partridges, and she can break into the government's mainframe in less than thirty seconds."

"What's with Hattie taking off her gloves, earrings, and headband?" Shelley asked.

"It's just one of her quirks. And much like her interest in tartan, we think it best not to ask," Oli answered.

"Honestly, how dim can the security team be?" Hattie remarked as she disarmed the alarm. "It took me all of twenty-two seconds to retrieve the code. They ought to be ashamed of themselves. Utterly ashamed."

Once through the door, the group met with yet another obstacle—a metal gate, secured with a thick lock and chain.

"It's bomb time," Oli said, motioning toward Darwin.

"Wait—did you say *bomb*?" Jonathan screeched.

"It's not a bomb; it's an explosive with a low volume," Darwin corrected Oli.

"That sounds a lot like a bomb to me," Jonathan mumbled.

"You needn't worry," Oli said to Jonathan.

"Darwin knows what he's doing. Blowing things up is his favorite pastime."

The so-called explosive with a low volume detonated, creating a sound similar to a balloon bursting, which was immediately followed by a thick plume of sulfurous smoke.

"Glasses? Khaki? Are you sure you're up for this?" Darwin asked. "Nina was our friend. She's far less likely to lash out at us than you."

"To put it bluntly, if she's going to infect anyone, it will be one of you, if not both of you," Oli clarified.

The thought of being more confused and less intelligent was nothing short of petrifying for Jonathan. And yet he knew that if he turned and hid in the boat, he wouldn't be able to live with himself.

"We're coming with you," Jonathan answered softly.

"See that, right there," Shelley said proudly, pointing to Jonathan. "That's why this guy is my hero eleven percent of the time."

"And the other eighty-nine percent of the time?" Hattie asked.

"Not even a little bit."

And on that note, Darwin motioned for the group to follow him down the cavernous black corridor into the Tower of London.

OCTOBER 23, 2:42 A.M. TOWER OF LONDON. LONDON, ENGLAND

Cold and drafty. The air thick with dampness and the faint smell of mildew. Soft scratching sounds reminded them that they were not alone. Scurrying through the corridors was nothing short of a parade of rodents. All in all, it was hardly a hospitable start to their journey.

"Good evening, sir," Darwin called out upon spotting a fast-approaching security guard. "I'm sure you're wondering what we're doing here. The answer is simple. It's none of your business." And with that, he lobbed what appeared to be a water balloon at the man's feet.

Splat.

The balloon exploded against the stone floor, mere inches from the guard's shoes. Seconds passed. He swayed back and forth. He stumbled. And finally, he collapsed.

"CHCl$_3$. The organic compound commonly known as chloroform knocks people unconscious rather rapidly," Darwin stated proudly before turning to Oli. "Would you be a gent and tie him up for me?"

"Tie him up? Absolutely not. I'm a historian, not a thug," Oli delivered dramatically.

"Such nonsense," Hattie said as she once again removed her gloves, earrings, and headband. "Personally, I've always found tying people up quite enjoyable."

"Um, I hate to break up the fun—" Jonathan interrupted.

"Total lie," Shelley chimed in. "Jonathan loves being a fun killer; it's part of his khaki personality."

"First of all, Shelley, I'm not a fun killer. And second of all—"

"Anyone who starts a sentence with 'first of all'... total fun killer... no question about it," Shelley stated confidently.

"What I was trying to say is, are we sure we want to tie up the security guard? What if we need help with Nina?" Jonathan asked.

"You cannot be serious! This lump of a man

would be utterly useless against Nina. She's a trained operative; he's just some nobody!" Hattie responded. "Honestly, the only thing he could do for us is fetch us a cup of tea, although on second thought, I doubt he could even do that. Very few people these days know how to make a *proper* cup of tea."

" 'Tea is one of the mainstays of civilization in this country and causes violent disputes over how it should be made,' " Oli quoted George Orwell while looking expectantly at the others, eager for someone to acknowledge his statement.

"Don't feel bad, it's a tough crowd," Jonathan whispered to Oli.

"I think it's best we split up so we can cover as much ground as possible," Darwin announced to the group as they approached an intersection of four hallways, each leading in a different direction. "Although, Khaki and Glasses should stay together. If they find Nina, they're going to need two brains just to stand a chance."

"I don't mean to be annoying, but I'm not really feeling the nickname Glasses," Shelley said with a playful shrug. "I've always been more of a Super Shelley or Shelltastic kind of girl."

"Here's the thing: I don't really care what you want to be called. I'm calling you Glasses, got it?" Darwin said, and then pointed at a nearby hall. "I'll take the northwest."

"Very well, then. I'll handle the southwest," Hattie said before pausing to adjust her headband and then disappearing down a dark corridor.

"I suppose the northeast is as good as any," Oli declared as he faded into the shadows.

"No problem, so I guess that means we're taking the... Wait, what's left? This is beginning to feel like one of those word problems that make my brain hurt," Shelley grumbled.

"This is the only corridor left, which means it's ours," Jonathan said. "Although, if I'm honest, I'm hoping we don't find Nina."

"Retract that statement right now, Johno! This is our time to shine! To show those book snakes what we're made of!"

"Book*worms*, not snakes," Jonathan corrected Shelley.

"I knew it was something that slithered."

"But what if Nina uses LIQ-30 on us?" Jonathan wondered aloud. "What would happen if we couldn't focus? We would be even more confused than we already are!"

"We'd be fine, just fine," Shelley lied as they started down the hall. "Is it just me or is it getting darker in here? Not that I'm afraid of the dark. Because spies can't be afraid of the dark. Can they? No, of course they can't! Although I'm starting to think *you* might be afraid of the dark. Don't worry, I'll slip my arm through yours to help keep you calm."

Jonathan rolled his eyes. "Thanks, Shells. Your arm is bringing me more comfort than you'll ever know."

"Did you feel that?" Shelley yelped.

"What? Did something bite you?"

"Bite me? You mean like a vampire? Do you think there are vampires in here?" Shelley asked.

"I meant like an insect," Jonathan clarified. "Vampires are not real."

"I have it on good authority that President Arons eats two cloves of garlic a day, just in case."

Jonathan sighed. "Please define what you mean by good authority."

"Well, if you really want to know—wait! What about *that*?"

"What?"

"The burst of cold air. Or as it is more commonly known, a ghost!"

"Ghosts, like vampires, are not real. Rogue teenage spies, however, are, so will you please start paying attention to the here and now and stop imagining supernatural visitors?" Jonathan implored Shelley as two hands grabbed hold of his shoulders and pushed him straight into a nearby pit.

"Shell—" Jonathan shrieked, although before he could even finish saying her name, she had landed on top of him.

Clink. Clink. Smash!

And just like that, a metal grate crashed down, imprisoning Jonathan and Shelley in a medieval pit.

"People always say that it's better to be lucky than smart, but if you aren't either, then what?"

—Joana Kreling, 11, Oklahoma City, Oklahoma

CHAPTER 7

<866383-JK-LOUC-236>

OCTOBER 23, 3:17 A.M. TOWER OF LONDON.
LONDON, ENGLAND

"Nina? Or should I say Friend-I-Haven't-Met-Yet?"
Shelley called out.

"If you'll talk to us, I think you'll realize that
we're not even worthy of being locked up," Jonathan said, his voice echoing from the bottom of the
deep stone pit, the sides smooth from centuries of
hands clawing at them in a desperate attempt to
escape. "We're just two nobodies!"

The sound of water diverted Jonathan's attention.

One then two then three then four and finally five streams slowly trickled into the pit, the flow growing stronger with each second that passed.

"Where's the water coming from?" Shelley shrieked. "We need to stop it or we'll drown!"

That's the idea, Jonathan thought. Nina, a girl he had never even met, was going to drown them. For what? For trying to stop her from poisoning ministers with LIQ-30. Did she really think them worthy of a watery grave? Jonathan began to shiver. His teeth chattered. His eyelids twitched. It was his body's way of revolting, of fighting against the inevitable—death.

Next to Jonathan, Shelley was jumping up and down as water pooled around their feet. "Please don't do this, Nina! We're good people! We recycle! We even bring our own bags to the grocery store!"

A dark figure moved through the room, jumping from shadow to shadow until finally exiting.

"Nina! Come back! Please!" Shelley screamed before noticing that her friend was now shaking uncontrollably as the water passed their knees.

How are we going to get out of here? Shelley

thought as she pulled at her hair, frustrated by the seeming impossibility of the situation.

"I've got it!" Shelley hollered, grabbing hold of Jonathan's shoulders. "Don't worry, I have a plan."

As the water neared his belly, Jonathan stammered, "I w-wish I could say that m-made me feel better, but your plans usually don't work."

"We're going to wait for the pit to fill with water, pushing us to the top, allowing us to open the metal grate," Shelley explained, eyes wide, anxiously waiting for Jonathan's reaction.

"You're a genius, Shelley Brown!" Jonathan exclaimed as he tried to give Shelley a hug.

"For real? Like they would let me into the genius club?" Shelley asked, her eyes alight with excitement as she imagined her parents' and sister's reaction to her becoming a certified genius.

"No, of course not," Jonathan answered, prompting Shelley to drop her head in disappointment.

"Come on, Shells! Don't be sad, you just saved our lives! Who cares if you're not an actual genius?" Jonathan said as the water continued to rise, bringing them closer and closer to the grate.

"That's easy for you to say. You're considered the smart one in your family!" Shelley responded.

"Can we put a pin in this conversation? Maybe it's the water or the medieval pit, but I'm having trouble concentrating," Jonathan explained as he extended his arm, his fingers grazing the metal grate. "Almost there!"

Second by second, the water brought them closer and closer, until they were finally able to grab hold of the cold metal bars.

"On the count of three. One...two...three," Jonathan instructed Shelley.

The realization was instantaneous: They didn't have the strength or momentum needed to push open something this heavy, not while treading water. Maybe not ever.

"It's impossible," Jonathan quietly admitted as he closed his eyes.

The water continued to rise, each drop bringing them closer to their deaths.

"I can't die, not now, not with the nickname Glasses," Shelley blubbered, tears rolling down her cheeks. "If I were some old person in a coma I wouldn't complain, and not just because people in comas can't talk! But this isn't fair—I'm too young! I've barely done anything on my to-do list!"

"Nina! Somebody! Help!" Jonathan screamed as Shelley continued babbling.

"Something's wrong...something's wrong..."

"Of course something's wrong—we're about to die!" Jonathan exploded.

"No! People always say that your life flashes before your eyes when you're about to die, kind of like a movie," Shelley said, her teeth chattering from fear.

"And?"

"It's not happening. I only see my future; all the things I'm supposed to do. All the things *we're* supposed to do," Shelley explained.

"I can't tell you how much I wish my head was filled with thoughts like that," Jonathan said, his eyes tearing up. "All I can see is my funeral. The empty chairs. My parents crying. The priest calling me Jack. Talk about an unexceptional end to an unexceptional life."

"Unexceptional? You're going to drown at the Tower of London while working as a spy!" Shelley retorted.

"Yeah, but no one will ever know that."

"I'll know it," Shelley responded.

"But you're going to die too."

It was a most unusual moment to smile, on the brink of death, and yet that's exactly what Jonathan and Shelley did.

"Yeah, I guess that's true," Shelley said as the sound of a match scratching, followed by a sudden burst of light, seized their attention.

"Dear, dear…this certainly does look like a pickle, now doesn't it?" Hattie announced in a slow, uneven manner as she leaned down over the pit, a candle in hand. "I suppose you are interested in a bit of help."

"Who, us? No way! We're really enjoying waiting for our lives to end!" Shelley hollered ferociously.

"You are? How interesting?" Hattie responded dreamily. "Did I ever tell you about the first time I made shepherd's pie? It was in August, which of course is a terrible month for vacationing, since everyone else is vacationing. Did we have dinner yet? I do loathe to skip meals. Although, it should be noted that I do not consider toast a meal. What was I saying again? Oh yes, marmalade. I make the best marmalade in England!"

"What's wrong with her?" Shelley asked, although she was pretty sure she already knew the answer.

"It appears our only hope for survival has been infected with LIQ-30," Jonathan answered as the water reached his chin. "It's not going to be easy, but we need to get her to focus."

"Hattie? I need you to lean down and pull this metal grate up, okay?" Shelley asked as calmly as she could, water sloshing into her mouth.

"You'd like to get out? I guess you have been in there an awfully long time. Say, what is that? A pool? Did I ever tell you about the summer Grandma taught her poodle Mitzi to swim?"

"Please!" Shelley interrupted. "Get us out of here!"

"Very well. I suppose I can try," Hattie answered, and then paused to remove her gloves, headband, and earrings. "Now then, what was I doing?"

"Opening the grate," Jonathan reminded the girl. "If you let us out, we could all go and have a cup of tea. Doesn't that sound nice?"

"Tea? What a wonderful idea! I'll put the kettle on, but it might take me a while, as I'm not at home right now," Hattie muttered, and exited the room.

"No! No! Come back!" Jonathan and Shelley yelled frantically. "Please! Don't leave!"

"That stupid clay-pigeon-shooting, cucumber-sandwich-eating redhead just left us here to die!" Shelley shrieked, and then paused when she heard the sound of footsteps. "Oh, thank heavens! Sweet, wonderful Hattie has come back for us!"

Only it wasn't Hattie.

"What's going on in here?" Darwin asked as he ran into the room.

"Get us out of here!" Shelley cried.

And that is exactly what Darwin did, freeing Jonathan and Shelley from certain death.

"Thank you," Jonathan uttered quietly as he and Shelley dragged themselves, soaking wet, from the pit.

"It's freezing in here," Shelley said, teeth chattering.

"Wait here. We've got dry clothes on the boat," Darwin said, and then dashed out of the room.

"Shells?"

"Yeah, Johno?"

"I'm really glad we're still alive."

"Me too. I definitely wasn't feeling the whole death-by-drowning part of my obituary."

"But if we have to die, I think we should die together," Jonathan added. "Then at least we'll die in the company of someone who knows what we've done with our lives. Someone who knows we were more than a couple of faceless classmates in the hall."

"We're somebodies, Johno, even if nobody knows it."

"Reach for the stars? But I can't
even touch the ceiling."

—Dax Winegarden, 12, San Rafael,
California

CHAPTER 8

<996901-DW-LOUC-958>

OCTOBER 23, 6:18 A.M. STREET. LONDON,
ENGLAND

"Hey, shorties," Hammett's unmistakable voice
called out as Jonathan and Shelley walked home,
dripping wet with prune-like skin and an over-
whelming sense of gratitude for the simple fact that
they were alive.

"Technically speaking, I'm tall for my age,"
Shelley responded as she turned to see Hammett
step out of a doorway.

"No, you're not; you're average," Jonathan chimed in.

"This guy," Shelley said, shaking her head. "He's the wrecking ball of dreams. Just knocking them down one by one. *You think you're tall, Shells? Think again!*"

"Come on, kiddo, don't tell me you actually thought you were tall for your age? You're not *that bad* a detective, are you?" Hammett asked, looking Jonathan and Shelley up and down. "You two were put through the ringer tonight, weren't you?"

"We almost drowned. My whole body looks like a raisin from being locked in a pit of water. Hattie was infected with LIQ-30. And as if all that wasn't bad enough, then Nina stole the boat, forcing us to walk home," Jonathan ranted.

"He's a real ray of sunshine, isn't he?" Hammett muttered to Shelley, toothpick dangling from his lips.

"Only if by *sunshine*, you mean that Johno burns your eyes, leaving you blind and in the dark," Shelley responded.

"Quite the smart aleck, aren't you?" Hammett said, winking at Shelley.

"I knew a man named Alec once," Nurse Maidenkirk said, stepping out from behind a nearby kiosk. "His left foot was removed due to gangrene. Then his right foot. Then his left hand. Then his—"

"Okay!" Hammett snapped. "We get the picture. They trimmed him nice and good like a rotten head of broccoli."

"Alec had peripheral artery disease, which stops the blood from reaching the limbs," Nurse Maidenkirk continued.

"And I thought I had a difficult partner," Jonathan mumbled to Hammett, who was looking unusually tense.

"These BAE operatives are like cough syrup; they might be helpful in the long run, but they leave a terrible taste in my mouth," Hammett grumbled. "The way they look at you two, like a couple of interlopers—"

"Is that a baby antelope? Because I hate it when people call baby animals by different names. Why aren't lambs called baby sheep? Or fawns baby deer? Why come up with a whole new name for them? It's like they're trying to confuse us!"

Jonathan and Hammett stared at Shelley, unsure what to make of her latest comments. As if suddenly understanding, Shelley nodded and smiled. "I see where you guys are going with this and I like it! Online petition to stop the use of baby animal names!"

"That is definitely not where I was going," Jonathan responded.

"Look here, kiddo, the only petition I'm signing is one that limits the amount of time we let you talk each day," Hammett said. "I'm no doctor, but I'm pretty sure you've got a case of gum-flapping disease. You just can't help yourself, can you?"

"I'm sensing you're not going to sign the petition, which means Khaki over here gets to be the first signature," Shelley said while turning animatedly to Jonathan.

"It's pretty unlikely I'll sign your petition," Jonathan said.

"How unlikely?" Shelley questioned.

"Joining-a-boy-band kind of unlikely."

"A boy band? No way. I've seen you dance. You're terrible. I'd start a petition to stop that from happening," Shelley said.

"Time's a-ticking here, kids," Hammett said, looking at his watch. "I've got someplace to be."

"As the saying goes, 'The early bird gets the

sunburn, so take your time and be a little late...or wear a hat.'"

"That is definitely *not* a saying," Jonathan said.

"Chocolate, anyone?" Nurse Maidenkirk interjected, offering Jonathan, Shelley, and Hammett a piece of her candy bar. "I once saw a dog drop dead seconds after fishing a box of chocolates out of the trash."

"Seconds?" Hammett questioned Nurse Maidenkirk. "I've never heard of chocolate affecting a dog so quickly."

"Well, it was either the chocolate or the car that jumped the curb and ran over the dog. They happened one after another, making it impossible to say for sure."

"This woman here, she's a certifiable wack job, you know that?" Hammett said fondly. "She spends her free days looking for bird bones in the park. But I keep her around; you want to know why? Because she's loyal, through and through. If I need her, she'll be there. She'll probably have a dead squirrel in her pocket, but she'll be there nonetheless."

Jonathan shrugged. "I guess you could consider that helpful."

"The being-there part or the dead squirrel?" Shelley asked.

"Listen up, this is serious!" Hammett instructed Jonathan and Shelley as he snapped his fingers. "You two are *so* alone in the world; not even the floor's going to be there if you fall."

"That's cold...colder than Antarctica...colder than Santa Claus's toes in the North Pole...although I bet Santa has pretty good boots," Shelley babbled.

Jonathan sighed. "Shelley's allergic to staying on topic."

"Hey," Hammett snapped. "Shelley may talk a lot of nonsense, but she's your partner and you need her."

"Did you hear that, Khaki? You need me!" Shelley said with a smug smile.

"And *you* need *him*. Average nobodies can get lost real easy in this world. And when they do, no one comes looking for them. Why? Because no one remembers they exist."

"Except our parents," Jonathan corrected Hammett. "They know we exist. They'd come looking for us."

"Your parents have been talking to a stuffed

animal for the last two days thinking it was you. Sure, you told them you were going away, but you think they remembered? Not a chance, kid. Not a chance."

"As the sunshine of my grandparents' lives," Shelley said, peering over her glasses to look at Hammett, "I can't imagine how lonely they are without me."

"Here's the bottom line, kid. Your grandparents know you're out of town. They just can't remember where you went. Your granddad suspects it has something to do with being dishonorably discharged from the Girl Scouts."

"Grandpa can't remember where I went, but he remembers that I was kicked out of the Girl Scouts for buying badges on the black market?" Shelley sputtered. "What is wrong with my family?!"

OCTOBER 23, 10:09 A.M. 10 DOWNING STREET. LONDON, ENGLAND

After arriving back at Downing Street at just past 6:30 in the morning, Jonathan and Shelley had quickly changed into their pajamas and climbed into their beds. However, less than four hours had

passed when Jonathan awoke with a start. Sure that he was still dreaming, he rubbed his eyes. But the face remained. Wrinkled, with a steady breath that smelled of strong tea and liquor. The woman was mere inches from the boy's face when she whispered.

"We're in the company of turncoats, I'm certain of it. They'll kill us if we stay. And they know how to make murder look like an accident."

"As much as I enjoy our little chats, Mrs. Cadogan, what do you say we limit our interactions to mealtimes?" Jonathan asked, the woman still inches from his face.

"They'll poison the food next."

"Have you woken up Shelley yet?" Jonathan asked.

"Who?"

"You know, my little blond friend?"

"You mean Gertrude? Poor thing, she was so terrified, she bit my arm and pushed me out of the room," Mrs. Cadogan explained.

"She bit you?" Jonathan said, barely containing his horror.

"That is not what happened," Shelley said with a huff, standing in the doorway.

"All right, then, what happened?" Jonathan responded, gently pushing Mrs. Cadogan away from his face.

"The old lady woke me from a very deep sleep, and as you can imagine, I was more than a little surprised to see *that face*," Shelley said, motioning toward Mrs. Cadogan. "At which time I might have accidentally placed my mouth on top of her arm in an effort to get her to leave my room."

"Children, you mustn't trust anyone. I've heard

95

that there are enemies on our soil, enemies who are trained in the art of deception," Mrs. Cadogan said ominously before pulling a piece of bread from the pocket of her dress.

"Nice breakfast," Shelley joked, pointing at the bread.

Eyes bulging, Mrs. Cadogan answered firmly, "We must all ration in wartime. It's our duty to the country."

"For someone who's supposed to be living off rations, you're looking a little on the plump side."

Clearly scandalized by Shelley's comment, Mrs. Cadogan gasped and then barked, "Are you insinuating that I am stealing other people's rations?"

"Shells, let's not upset the old lady with dementia."

"Fine," Shelley acquiesced. "I'll issue a retraction."

OCTOBER 23, 2:08 P.M. BAE HEADQUARTERS. LONDON, ENGLAND

Randolph stood in the center of the austere room, his arms crossed, his brow furrowed, and his mouth frowning. The news of Jonathan and Shelley's near-death experience had rattled him. He knew the truth: They were nothing more than a couple of kids whose strongest asset was that they were forgettable. Was it possible that they were in over their heads? That President Arons had misjudged their abilities?

"Good afternoon, Teeth. Khaki and Glasses aren't in yet?" Darwin called out as he walked into headquarters.

"Khaki and Glasses?" Randolph repeated.

"Come on, Teeth, you know who I'm talking about. Bob and Sheila."

"Who?" Randolph responded.

"The American operatives."

"I believe the names you are looking for are Jonathan and Shelley," Randolph informed Darwin, motioning toward the left side of the room.

"We're right here," Jonathan said, standing up.

"That's weird. I mistook you two for chairs," Darwin said.

"Unfortunately, being mistaken for office furniture happens more often than I care to admit," Jonathan said as Shelley shook her head.

"I've been mistaken for a bench, sure. A desk once or twice, but your common office chair? Never!" Shelley said with a huff.

"My sincere apologies, Glasses," Darwin offered with a smirk.

"So you're sticking with Glasses. Are you sure you don't want to give Super Shelley or Shelltastic a try?"

"I don't think so," Darwin responded as Oli entered the room, Hattie trailing behind him with a newspaper in hand.

"A three-letter word for *feline*?" Hattie mumbled to herself as she took a seat. "This chair is terribly uncomfortable. Personally I've always been fond of hard beds and soft chairs. And ice cream. I love ice cream."

"Look at her, Teeth!" Darwin blustered. "She's struggling to do the crossword and it's not even the weekend edition!"

"Hattie was a million times smarter than we are and now look at her," Jonathan whispered to Shelley. "If Nina infects us, we're pretty much done."

"If I become any less focused than I already am, I'm pretty sure my parents will downgrade me to niece or cousin. Just to save face," Shelley admitted.

"It's not easy being the only non-genius in a family of geniuses, is it, Shells?"

"It's like riding a bicycle when you only have one

leg. Seriously hard," Shelley said solemnly before breaking into a smile. "Although, if everyone in my family were infected with LIQ-30, I would be the smartest one. The top of the food chain, not that I would eat them, because I'm not a cannibal. Although, if you leave me in the woods long enough with a dead body, I could be swayed. But only if there was barbecue sauce."

"This conversation just got really weird. And not in a good way. In an I'm-definitely-going-to-lock-my-bedroom-door-tonight kind of way," Jonathan said as Randolph huddled with Darwin and Oli in the corner.

"Relax, I would never eat you. You're too skinny. It wouldn't be worth all the effort to make a fire, marinate you. Okay, I'm starting to see what you were saying about the conversation getting weird."

After a few seconds, Randolph stepped away from Darwin and Oli, who then lured Hattie down to the cafeteria with the promise of milk and cookies.

"I hope you don't mind, but I asked them to step out for a moment so that we might have a talk," Randolph said, motioning for Jonathan and Shelley to take seats at a nearby table.

"I must admit that after hearing of your near-death experience last night, my first reaction was to pull you from the field. To send you back to America on the next plane. But then I got to thinking about President Arons's great faith in you and your ability to move through life without registering on anyone's radar," Randolph explained.

"That's what we're known for, by the few people who remember us, anyway," Jonathan said.

"It's true that there is something about you two that makes you slip one's mind," Randolph admitted.

"What are you guys talking about? Tons of people remember me," Shelley interjected.

"Unfortunately, the truth hurts Shelley so much that she refuses to accept it," Jonathan explained to Randolph. "It's not an easy road to walk, that of the forgotten child."

"Forgotten *child*? More like forgotten *young lady*!" Shelley corrected Jonathan.

"So now you're admitting you're forgettable?"

"What does it matter if I admit it or not? Can't you just let me be happy for a minute? There's no reason to blow out the candle inside me."

"The candle inside you?" Jonathan repeated with a chuckle.

"What? You're the only one who gets to talk like some lame poem inside a greeting card? *The forgotten child!*"

"All right now," Randolph interrupted, sensing that the situation was snowballing out of control. "After much consideration, we have decided to use the two of you to collect updates from our eyes, that is, our informants, around the city."

"You mean undercover operatives?" Shelley asked.

"No. These are people who have either come forward of their own volition to help us with tips, or, more likely, they were caught committing a crime and have agreed to act as informants as a means to avoid jail time. Either way, it's crucial that they remain undercover, which is where you two come in. Since you're rarely, if ever, noticed, we thought you perfect for the job."

Shelley nodded and then pushed her smudged glasses up the bridge of her nose. "This is good to know in case I'm ever arrested. Not that I'm planning on doing anything illegal. Not this year, anyway."

"In order to protect the identities of our informants, we do not maintain photographic records of them, instead giving each one a unique signal by which our operatives can identify them," Randolph said as he pushed a pen and paper across the desk to Shelley.

"Pen? Paper? What is this, 1995? All I need is this up here," Shelley said, tapping the side of her head. "You're looking at a state-of-the-line computer."

"Shells, why don't we write it down—"

Shelley threw up her right hand to silence Jonathan. "Every five minutes, you know what my brain is doing?"

"I'm afraid to even ask," Jonathan muttered.

"Autosaving, just in case the computer crashes."

"In third grade Priscilla Wood
called me a weirdo. It was
the best day of my life. I had
finally made an impression on
someone!"

—Evelyn Ward, 13, Chattanooga, Tennessee

CHAPTER 9

<958800-EW-LOUC-521>

OCTOBER 23, 3:07 P.M. STREET. LONDON, ENGLAND

"I'm sensing someone could use a hug," Shelley offered, arms extended as she walked down the street next to Jonathan.

"No thanks."

"And by *someone*, I mean me," Shelley said as she pulled Jonathan in for a painfully close hug. "I'm petrified. I'm sweating like a pig about to go to slaughter."

"That's graphic," Jonathan said as he pried himself from Shelley's grasp.

"I know how much you look up to me, Johno, so I've been trying to be strong for you," Shelley said, her voice crumbling. "But I don't think I can do it anymore."

"First of all—"

"What did I tell you about saying things like 'first of all'?" Shelley cut in.

"Fine," Jonathan grumbled. "What I was trying to say is, I don't look up to you, which isn't to say that I look down on you. I just look *at* you."

Shelley nodded.

"But I get being scared," Jonathan admitted. "Trust me, I'm terrified. What if Nina infects us and then we're too dumb to be spies?"

"Never speak those words again! We're going to find her and stop LIQ-30 before it goes viral...and not in a cool video way...but in a scary outbreak way...."

"Yeah, I got that."

OCTOBER 23, 3:47 P.M. BUCKINGHAM PAL-ACE. LONDON, ENGLAND

Buckingham Palace, home to the queen of England, was surrounded by a tall and imposing gate that was monitored twenty-four hours a day by guards. Ten feet from the gate, amid the throngs of tourists, Jonathan and Shelley eyed the lineup of guards carefully.

"Randolph said the informant would be wearing a black furry hat," Shelley recalled as she racked her brain for more information.

"Shells, all the guards are wearing black furry hats."

"And a red jacket!" Shelley screeched excitedly.

"Are you looking at the same people I am?" Jonathan asked. "They're all in red jackets. Every single one of them!"

"I guess we have no choice but to go up and ask which one of them is the undercover informant," Shelley suggested. "Sometimes, honesty really is the only policy."

"Undercover informants do not tell people they are undercover informants!"

Shelley paused. "You might be right about that," she accepted, rubbing her chin.

"Plus, my guidebook says the guards are forbidden to speak to anyone."

"Well, my guidebook says the guards are part

of a cult who are waiting for their leader's return, hence the furry hats. Their leader is an intergalactic bear. Okay, I made that up. I just really wanted a fact that could outdo your fact."

Jonathan rolled his eyes and then sighed, "I think it's time to call Randolph and admit that we forgot what he told us and that we should have written down his instructions instead of pretending to have good memories."

"I would rather swim back to America than admit we can't even remember a few simple things!"

"I hate to point fingers, but you were the one who said your brain was better than a computer's hard drive, that nothing could be erased from your mind," Jonathan recalled, much to Shelley's aggravation.

"Excuse me, kiddos, but would you mind taking a photo of me and the missus?" a man asked, prompting Jonathan and Shelley to look up.

Standing before them, dressed in jeans and sweatshirts with cameras dangling around their necks, were none other than Hammett and Nurse Maidenkirk.

"Here's our camera, kid," Hammett instructed Jonathan. "All you need to do is look through the lens."

"I'm actually not a very good photographer. I have a tendency to cut off people's heads or feet," Jonathan conceded.

"Just look through the lens, kid," Hammett insisted.

And when Jonathan finally did, he found a message. THIRD FROM THE LEFT.

"But how could you possibly know?"

"He's the only one who noticed the two of you

standing here arguing," Hammett said quietly before raising his voice. "Thanks for the picture. Enjoy the rest of your vacation."

"It's the third guard from the left," Jonathan informed Shelley as she watched Hammett and Nurse Maidenkirk disappear into the crowd.

"I don't want to say I'm psychic...but I had a feeling it was the third guy from the left."

"And yet you said nothing while we were standing here, searching our brains for some small detail to help us figure out who was the informant," Jonathan responded.

"You are what is known as a psychic hater."

"Great," Jonathan said. "You can add it to the list after fun killer, Negative Ned, sunshine sponge..."

Shelley snapped her fingers. "Get it together, Johno. We have work to do," she said, then started toward the informant.

"Hey there, furry-hat man," Shelley whispered. "Seen anything fishy? And by *fishy*, I don't mean an aquarium."

The guard stared straight ahead, seemingly unaware of Shelley.

"Is he ignoring me? Or does he just not hear me?"

"Let me try," Jonathan said, leaning into the guard. "Seen anything?"

"Negative," the man replied, most impressively, without even moving his lips.

"Come on, Shells, we have two more stops to make," Jonathan said as he turned to leave.

"Just one thing," Shelley said before grabbing the guard's arm. "I hope no bears were killed or injured in the making of that hat."

Jonathan sighed. "The part-time vegetarian strikes again."

OCTOBER 23, 4:36 P.M. THE LONDON ZOO. LONDON, ENGLAND

The zoo was crowded. Children as far as the eye could see. Jonathan and Shelley navigated the strollers like land mines, stealthily moving out of the way every time a double-wide, titanium-plated beast barreled toward them.

"There should be a law against double-wide strollers," Jonathan griped. "They're nothing but a public nuisance!"

"What about slow walkers? Unless they're really

old or injured, there's no acceptable excuse," Shelley said before turning her attention to something in the gorilla compound.

"Shells? What is it?" Jonathan asked.

"I think this might be love at first sight."

"You're in love with a gorilla?"

"No! He's in love with me! Look at the way he's staring at me," Shelley said, grinning from ear to ear.

"It must be rewarding to finally be noticed— even if it is by another species."

Shelley grabbed Jonathan's arm. "We've got eyes on us, and I'm not talking about my new friend."

"A gorilla looks at you for a couple of seconds and suddenly he's your friend?"

"To the left of the gate, there's a woman in a khaki outfit," Shelley whispered while pretending to read the sign posted in front of the gorillas' cage.

"The woman is to the right of the gate, not the left," Jonathan corrected Shelley.

"What is this obsession with right and left? Is there really that big of a difference?"

"Actually, yes, there—"

"She's signaling us!"

"You remember the signal?" Jonathan asked with genuine surprise.

"No, of course not," Shelley replied impatiently. "But she's waving us over, which is a universal signal for 'Hey, I want to talk to you.'"

Shelley waved good-bye to her new "friend," prompting Jonathan to shake his head, before approaching the middle-aged woman with frizzy hair and brown, leathery skin.

"You guys are friends of one-eyed Randy?"

Jonathan and Shelley nodded.

"Then what's the problem? I've been signaling you for almost four minutes now."

"My friend here forgot the signal," Shelley said, motioning to Jonathan.

"What kind of operatives forget the signal? I've never heard of such a thing!" the woman barked at Jonathan and Shelley.

"He recently suffered a head injury that has impacted his short-term memory," Shelley said, eyeing the woman closely. "Don't feel guilty. How were you to know? Yes, you hurt his feelings, there might even be a few tears later—"

"There's no crying in espionage!" Jonathan

burst out before giving the woman a tell-us-what-you-got kind of look.

"There was a break-in, someone stole a tranquilizer gun, that's it."

"Got it," Shelley said to the woman. "You were caught committing a crime, weren't you? That's how you wound up as an informant, isn't it?"

"Shells, I think someone's following us. We need to move," Jonathan said in a brusque manner as he pulled her away from the cage. "I've noticed an orange hat trailing behind us since we entered the zoo. At first I thought it was a coincidence, but we've moved around so much that it can't be."

Walking at a brisk yet inconspicuous pace, Jonathan and Shelley started making their way through the throngs of people.

"Casually glance behind us and tell me if you see someone with an orange baseball cap," Jonathan instructed Shelley.

"You got it," Shelley replied, then dropped to her knees. "My ankle, my ankle!"

"This is your idea of casual?" Jonathan grumbled.

"The orange cap is still on our tail," Shelley said

as Jonathan helped her back onto her feet. "Do you think it's Nina?"

"It's possible that she's come to finish what she started yesterday."

"Why would anyone want to kill us? We're such good people," Shelley whined.

"Because we're trying to stop her and she believes what she's doing is more important than a couple of nobodies' lives," Jonathan said as he scanned the path ahead for an exit.

"Nobodies count too!" Shelley cried dramatically, pumping her fist in the air. "Just because no one remembers our names doesn't mean you can kill us!"

"We don't know that the person in the orange cap is Nina. For all we know, she's working with other people and she's sent one of them to get us," Jonathan said.

"I'm not going to just wait around for her to take another shot at us," Shelley said, suddenly turning and charging full speed, or more precisely, as fast as an unathletic kid can, toward the person in the orange cap.

Arms flailing. Legs jutting out. There was no hiding Shelley's physical awkwardness.

"You're going down!" Shelley hollered as she rammed into the person with the orange cap with all her might.

"Ahhhh!" a young girl's voice cried out. "Help me! Somebody help me!"

Upon hearing the girl's terrified voice, Jonathan looked around and suddenly noted the smattering of orange caps all around the zoo. Much like a lightning bolt, the truth of the situation hit Jonathan with such force that he was momentarily paralyzed.

After regaining control of his body, Jonathan ran toward Shelley, wailing, "It's a field trip! It's a field trip!"

"Tell me where Nina is!" Shelley hollered at the frightened girl.

"I made a mistake!" Jonathan screamed in between gasps of air. "A bunch of kids are wearing orange caps as part of a field trip!"

Glistening with perspiration, Shelley immediately let go of the young girl. "I'm really sorry. This seems to have been a case of poor detective work on my partner's behalf. Is there any chance you'd be willing to accept a full retraction of my behavior?"

"What? I can't hear you," the girl responded as Jonathan grabbed Shelley's arm.

"She called for reinforcements! Run!" Jonathan shrieked as a mass of orange hats descended upon them.

OCTOBER 23, 5:33 P.M. TATE BRITAIN. LONDON, ENGLAND

"What do you say we keep the whole tackling-of-a-young-child story to ourselves?" Jonathan asked sheepishly as the two walked up the steps to the palatial entrance to the Tate Britain Museum.

"Is someone feeling guilty that their substandard detective work led to the emotional scarring of a poor, innocent girl?" Shelley asked, peering judgmentally over the frames of her glasses at Jonathan.

"I never told you to tackle the girl. You just took off. You didn't even give me a heads-up," Jonathan responded. "So I think it's only fair that we share the guilt fifty-fifty."

"Fine," Shelley conceded. "Plus, it wasn't that

bad. At least she has an interesting story. I've been waiting my whole life for an interesting story."

"Shells, twenty years from now, I'm pretty sure that girl is going to be telling this story to a therapist," Jonathan said, shaking his head.

"I've been waiting my whole life for a therapist. Someone who has to listen to me whether they want to or not because they're being paid? Dream come true."

OCTOBER 23, 5:42 P.M. J.M.W. TURNER EXHIBIT, TATE BRITAIN. LONDON, ENGLAND

Huddled in front of paintings, men and women conversed in a hushed yet serious manner. It was a strange thing about museums, but much like one's elderly aunt, they demanded good behavior. And in the many decades since the museum had opened, the Tate Britain had rarely faced an incident more irksome than a tourist snapping their gum or texting while walking—but then again, that was before Jonathan and Shelley arrived.

"Shells, were you able to find the details of this mission on your hard drive?" Jonathan asked, stifling a laugh as they entered the J.M.W. Turner exhibit.

"So I exaggerated my memory capabilities a little," Shelley said, looking around the room. "Big deal. I remember the important bits, like that there's a flash drive hidden behind a painting by some guy named Turner."

"But which painting?"

"The one by Turner," Shelley responded impatiently.

"Shells, maybe the sign on the wall isn't clear enough for you, but this whole exhibit is by J.M.W. Turner."

"So we'll look under every painting," Shelley answered nonchalantly.

"There are people everywhere," Jonathan said as he scanned the room.

"It appears you may have a point," Shelley said, rubbing her chin before suddenly snapping her fingers. "You know what clears a room in less than a minute?"

"I'm afraid to ask."

"Fire!" Shelley said proudly. "People hate fire."

"You're suggesting we start a fire in a museum? Are you insane?" Jonathan asked.

"Relax, Dr. Downer, I'm talking about pulling the fire alarm and tricking everyone into thinking there's a fire when there's not."

"While that's preferable to starting an actual fire, I still have a bad feeling about this," Jonathan said.

"But you have a bad feeling about everything."

"That's true," Jonathan acknowledged. "Sometimes, just waking up gives me a bad feeling. Is that normal?"

"No, but unfortunately we don't have time to deal with your emotional baggage right now. We have a building to clear," Shelley said as she slipped her hands into her oversized trench coat and started skulking around the exhibit, carefully scanning the walls for a fire alarm.

"Johno," Shelley said, "check out three o'clock."

"The guy in the green sweater?" Jonathan responded.

"No! That's eleven o'clock."

"How is that eleven o'clock?"

"Oh, forget it," Shelley said with a huff. "See

that small red square on the wall next to the door? That's a fire alarm."

"Again, I have a really bad feeling about this plan," Jonathan reiterated.

"Which is why I think you should pull the fire alarm."

"No way."

"Haven't you ever heard the saying 'He who doubts the plan must use his hand to execute the plan'?"

"First of all, you just made up that saying. I can tell because it makes absolutely no sense. And second of all, I'm never going to do it. And by *never*, I mean making-the-dean's-list kind of never."

Shelley released a long Jonathan-worthy sigh, threw her hands up in the air, and relented. "Fine, I'll do it, you big baby!"

Strutting across the room, weaving in and out of tourists, Shelley exuded the kind of inexplicable confidence that Jonathan couldn't help but envy. To feel strong and self-assured while walking straight into the unknown: That was impressive. Or insane. Or both, Jonathan thought as he watched Shelley nonchalantly pull the small red lever marked FIRE.

Thunderous sirens blared. A frenetic strobe light flashed. People scattered, desperate to find the closest exit. And watching it all, a smile draped across her face, was Shelley.

A job well done, or so she thought. For just as Shelley prepared to take a bow, a security guard appeared before her, red-faced and visibly angry.

"Why did you pull the fire alarm?" the man screamed over the sirens.

Shelley couldn't help but smile, flattered that someone other than a gorilla had taken notice of her.

"I said, why did you pull the fire alarm!" the man repeated just as the sirens ceased. "Young lady, you're going to need to come with me." He grabbed hold of Shelley's arm.

"See that boy with the black hair plastered to his head? That's my friend. And wherever I go, he goes."

Jonathan sighed. "I'm pretty sure this policy is going to land me in jail one day."

"I'm beginning to think that making friends is harder to achieve than world peace."

—Dolly Smythe, 11, Phoenicia, New York

CHAPTER 10

<274830-DS-LOUC-982>

OCTOBER 23, 5:59 P.M. BACK ROOM, TATE BRITAIN. LONDON, ENGLAND

"I've got to tell you guys, I've been interrogated before, but never in a room this nice," Shelley said as she took in the beige sofas and potted plants.

Jonathan nodded in agreement while seated next to Shelley on one of the sofas.

"Is that lavender I smell? With just a hint of—"

"Miss?" an overweight bald man interrupted Shelley. "My colleague informs me that you pulled the fire alarm in the Turner exhibit. Is that correct?"

"Yes, that is correct," Shelley confirmed, leaning back against the sofa.

"Sit up!" Jonathan hissed.

"Relax, Khaki, I got this."

"And you did this because you thought it would be funny? Perhaps in some misguided attempt to impress this young man over here?" the bald man continued.

"Impress Jonathan? Why would I need to do that? This kid worships me!"

"I think *worship* is a bit of an exaggeration. I like you, most of the time. Although sometimes you really annoy me," Jonathan answered honestly.

"Here's the thing, Officer—can I call you Officer?" Shelley continued, completely ignoring Jonathan's comments.

"No, you may call me Mr. Phillips."

"Mr. Phillips, I smelled smoke. And as the concerned citizen I am, I didn't want to waste a second. Because as any good fireman or -woman will tell you, hesitation costs lives," Shelley stated theatrically.

Mr. Phillips narrowed his eyes at Shelley and said, "I find your story highly suspect."

"Well, I find your whole outfit highly suspect!"

"Mr. Phillips," Jonathan screeched loudly in an effort to drown out Shelley. "My friend is not very smart. Sure she wears glasses and looks like a nerd. But the truth is, she's a real dud in the classroom," Jonathan continued as he pulled his pocket-sized version of *How to Make Great Popcorn in the Microwave* from his jacket. "As a matter of fact, I just so happen to have a copy of Shelley's report card with me, if you would be so kind as to take a look."

Mr. Phillips begrudgingly took the report card from Jonathan and began to read it aloud. " 'A profoundly disappointing student…the inability to logically reason bars advancement in mathematics.…Middle-of-the-road results are the best-case scenario for Shelley.' "

"It's almost tragic, isn't it?" Jonathan uttered.

Mr. Phillips turned toward Shelley and offered a condescending smile. "We can't all be special, now can we? Poor thing, you really were trying to help."

OCTOBER 23, 6:38 P.M. STREET. LONDON, ENGLAND

"Any time you want to thank me, by all means, go ahead," Jonathan said as the two walked away from the Tate Britain, albeit without the flash drive they had intended to pick up.

"You expect me to thank you for humiliating me? And to think, you call *me* crazy," Shelley said, eyes pricking with tears.

The voice in the back of Shelley's head, the one she tried so hard to block out, grew louder by the second. *It's not Jonathan's fault; he didn't write the report. Your teachers did, which means it's all true. You're a no one, Shelley. A dim-witted no one.*

Shelley's shoulders hunched forward, her head dropped, and she closed her eyes.

"Are you okay?"

"You don't know how lucky you are that your parents are dumb. It's awful to be the only dunce in a family of geniuses," Shelley sputtered.

"I prefer the term *intellectually challenged*, rather than *dumb*, when it comes to my parents. And you're not a dunce, Shells."

"Yes, I am. You heard the report."

"That report is just one small fraction of who you are. Fine, maybe you're not good at math or history. But you're good at other things, things they don't write about in those reports," Jonathan said, placing his arm around Shelley's shoulders.

"Like what?"

"You have a wild imagination," Jonathan answered. "Remember the time you told me that you wanted to come back as a sloth in your next life so you could nap every twenty-five to thirty minutes?"

"Sloths rule," Shelley said quietly before adding, "I guess my imagination is pretty unique."

"And you're an optimist. You look on the bright side of everything. A raccoon dies in a garbage can and you think, *Hey, at least he died doing what he loved—eating trash.* As a lifelong pessimist, I know firsthand what a difference optimism can make."

Shelley's shoulders relaxed. She lifted her head, wiped away her tears, and cracked the faintest of smiles. This was yet another great thing about Shelley: She recovered quickly.

"Who am I kidding? I'm incredible, aren't I?" Shelley declared as she transitioned into her superhero stance—shoulders back, hands on hips.

"You're amazing, Shells. And I mean that."

"Would you say I'm your own personal role model? Someone you think of in times of struggle?"

Jonathan couldn't help but smile. "If it makes you feel better, sure, why not."

OCTOBER 23, 8:12 P.M. BAE HEADQUARTERS. LONDON, ENGLAND

Randolph appeared more disheveled than usual. Slightly matted on the sides, his hair was in need of a brushing. Pacing back and forth in front of Jonathan, Shelley, Darwin, Oli, and Hattie, he emitted an anxious air. Not that Jonathan and Shelley were focused on Randolph's stressed demeanor; they were far too preoccupied with his glass eye, which was currently stuck looking down at his nose.

"Teeth, I'm quite certain that Nina is going to make contact with the ministers—namely those from Sussex and Kent—soon, as the vote to drill in nature preserves is fast approaching."

"You needn't worry, Darwin. Security measures are already in place," Randolph answered as he continued to pace.

"Why didn't you tell us?"

"Because I'm your boss and because you continue to call me Teeth!" Randolph barked.

"What is the plural of *Teeth*? *Teeves*?" Hattie asked from the corner of the room.

"*Teeth* is the plural of *tooth*, remember?" Jonathan answered, inwardly thrilled to finally be able to correct a BAE agent.

"Ah, yes, that's right," Hattie said before resuming her newfound hobby of staring off into space.

"Remember, Randolph," Oli said as he stood up. " 'It ain't what they call you, it's what you answer to.' W. C. Fields."

"Come on, Teeth, you're making too big a deal of it. You don't hear Glasses or Khaki complaining, do you?" Darwin said.

"Actually, I've complained," Shelley stated, pushing her glasses up the bridge of her nose. "Quite extensively, as a matter of fact."

"Your name is Teeth?" Hattie asked Randolph as she fingered her pearl necklace. "Dear me, I do believe I've been calling you by the wrong name for quite some time. Not to worry, Teeth, I shall make it up to you with a mince pie. Or a chocolate bar. I love chocolate, don't you? Wait. What was I talking about? Ah, yes, cavities. They're dreadful, aren't they?"

Eyes bulging with fear, Jonathan leaned in and whispered to Shelley, "One drop of bat saliva and I'll make my parents look like Nobel Prize winners."

"My name is not Teeth!" Randolph snapped at Hattie before regaining his composure. "My apologies, Hattie, I know you are not yourself these days."

"I think someone needs a hug, maybe even two," Shelley said as she approached Randolph, arms extended.

"The situation must be very dire, for that does not sound entirely horrendous," Randolph said as he dabbed his perspiring brow with a monogrammed handkerchief. "The prime minister is losing patience. We need to find Nina before she infects someone else."

"We all want to find Nina," Oli replied. "We just haven't a clue where to look."

"Why don't Johno and I check out Nina's dorm room? Maybe we'll find something you guys missed," Shelley said.

"I don't think that's necessary," Oli responded curtly. "We were very thorough. We are, after all, professionals."

"As are we," Jonathan pointed out.

"I don't see any harm in letting the Americans give the room another glance," Randolph declared, prompting Oli and Darwin to exchange tense looks.

The BAE boys' reaction piqued Jonathan's and Shelley's curiosity. Were they really that competitive? Or could it be something else?

OCTOBER 24, 10:00 A.M. EVERGREEN BOARD-ING SCHOOL. LONDON, ENGLAND

Weathered limestone buildings surrounded by perfectly manicured hedges made up the campus of Evergreen Boarding School. Formal with a hint of stuffiness, the ambiance immediately rubbed Shelley the wrong way.

"Is it me or are these kids looking down their perfect little noses at us?" Shelley asked Jonathan as the two made their way toward boardinghouse number three.

"How could they be judging us when they don't even see us?" Jonathan replied.

"You may have a point," Shelley conceded before looking up at the gray sky. "This weather makes me think global warming might not be such a bad thing."

Jonathan ignored Shelley entirely, which in and of itself was not such an extraordinary thing. After all, listening to her blather on all day long was no easy feat. However, on this particular occasion Jonathan had not zoned out, but rather zoomed in—on two people, to be precise.

"I know you're probably not going to believe me after the incident at the zoo, but someone's following us," Jonathan announced.

"Let me guess—you've noticed a girl in a red-and-gray uniform trailing us," Shelley said with a smirk as she looked around the quad teeming with girls in red-and-gray uniforms.

"No, it's Darwin and Oli," Jonathan said as he looked across the lawn. "Only they keep losing sight of us. Trailing unexceptionals is hard work, even for trained professionals."

"They're worried we're going to find something they missed, which makes me really hope we do!"

A wooden bed. A dresser. And a closet. Nina's
dorm room was a stale and impersonal space, bar-
ring a couple of plants and photos.

"Ferns remind me of doctors' offices and *li-
berries*. Two places I've never cared to spend a lot of
time," Shelley said as Jonathan shook his head and
resisted the urge to tell his friend that the word was
actually *libraries*.

While looking at the potted plants along the
windowsill, Shelley noticed a picture of Nina's
grandmother in front of a bakery. "This must be the
place mentioned in the e-mail, Petit Four and Petit
More."

"Hmm," Jonathan said as he opened the closet
doors.

"What does *hmm* mean?"

"Aerosol cans are terrible for the environment,"
Jonathan said as he held up aerosol deodorant, hair
spray, and room freshener.

"Obviously, Nina doesn't know that."

"Shells, if *I* know that they're bad for the environment, trust me, Nina knows."

"Then maybe she confiscated them from other people, sort of like what I've been trying to do with your khaki pants collection."

"Maybe," Jonathan muttered as he spotted the trash can in the corner.

The medium-sized wicker basket was overflowing with crumpled papers, a couple of half-eaten sandwiches, and a slew of empty soda cans.

"Shells, something isn't right. A radical environmentalist who doesn't recycle aluminum cans and uses aerosol deodorant and hair spray? I don't think so."

Shelley's eyes widened. "Are you thinking what I'm thinking?"

"I just told you what I was thinking. Remember?"

"How much easier would life be if we could read each other's minds? Although, reading your mind could also be seriously boring, like, I'm getting tired just thinking about it."

"Shells?"

"Yeah, Johno?"

"Will you please just tell me what you were thinking?"

"We should pay Nina's grandma a visit. They seem close; she could know something."

"That's *actually* a good idea."

Shelley smiled and then playfully punched Jonathan's shoulder. "Don't feel bad. I'm sure one day, you'll have one too."

"Everyone has silly, half-baked
ideas; I just happen to share
mine with the world."

—Joshua Bowyer, 11, Brunswick, Vermont

CHAPTER 11

`<702345-JB-LOUC-564>`

OCTOBER 24, 2:35 P.M. MRS. MITFORD'S
HOUSE. CASTLE COMBE, ENGLAND

"I hope you don't find this inappropriate," Shelley
said to Mrs. Mitford, Nina's well-maintained grandmother, over tea in the sitting room. "But you smell
really good, like butter cookies and cinnamon."

"Thank you, dear," Mrs. Mitford responded
as she fiddled with a loose string coming out of the
sofa. "I must admit I have something of a sweet
tooth, always have. I can't quite explain it, but biscuits and cakes bring me such happiness."

"You know what makes me happy? Popping open a Coke and jamming on my air guitar," Shelley said.

"I don't follow," Mrs. Mitford said, clearly confused by Shelley's ramblings.

"No one does," Jonathan interjected. "Now, about Nina. Was she always passionate about the environment? Or was this a cause she took up recently?"

"The environment? You mean the outdoors?" Mrs. Mitford chuckled. "Nina loathes nature. She's absolutely petrified of spiders and insects. As a child she used to cover her room in insect repellent. The whole house smelled like a chemical plant."

"So Nina's not into camping, but she's dedicated, maybe even a little extreme, when it comes to protecting the planet from pollution and deforestation?" Jonathan pressed on.

"Nina would never help a corporation destroy the rain forest or drop chemicals in a river, but that's not to say she gives much thought to such things," Mrs. Mitford said, pausing to smile. "It was nothing short of a miracle when I finally convinced her to put her water bottles in the recycling and not the bin. Teenagers can be very lazy, as your parents will soon learn."

"I know how you feel. My parents are actually pretty lazy themselves," Jonathan added.

"So Nina wasn't a tree hugger? She didn't yell at people who wasted paper or left the tap running while they brushed their teeth?" Shelley asked, clearly confused by the conflicting reports on Nina.

"Oh, the shower! Nina leaves the water running for five minutes straight before getting in. She likes it to feel like a steam room," Mrs. Mitford said with a laugh. "She really is such a wonderful girl—but a conservationist she is not."

Jonathan couldn't help but furrow his brow. The situation was starting to give him a headache. How was it that Nina's coworkers and family had such different ideas about the girl? Who, if anyone, knew the real Nina?

"And just to be clear, you're close to your grand-daughter, right?" Jonathan asked.

"Very close," Mrs. Mitford answered before adding, "These are most peculiar questions. Where did you say you were from again?"

"The Evergreen school paper. We're doing a profile on Nina in our next issue," Shelley explained.

"Well then, you ought to interview that boy she's always talking about…Charles…no…David…no…Darwin, yes, that's it. Darwin, like the evolutionist."

Jonathan nodded apprehensively. "We'll be sure to do that."

OCTOBER 24, 4:48 P.M. TRAIN STATION. LONDON, ENGLAND

"Maybe the old lady just thinks she's close to her granddaughter," Shelley said to Jonathan as they stepped off the train and into a crowd of commuters trying to make their way home. "After all, teenagers hide things from their parents, so why not their grandparents?"

"Teenagers hide *bad* things, not recycling and trying to save the planet."

"But Nina's a spy. Spies are not just professional liars, they're professional secret keepers," Shelley reasoned.

"I don't know, Shells. There's something about this that doesn't feel right."

Shelley lowered her glasses and looked Jonathan in the eye. "When something smells funky, check the aquarium, because your fish is probably dead."

"What does that mean?"

"It means that when you think something's wrong, it probably is. Or it just means that your fish is dead and it's time to flush it," Shelley explained as she stepped out of the way of a particularly fast-walking commuter.

"Your fish died? Would you like me to perform an autopsy?" a familiar voice interrupted from behind, prompting Jonathan and Shelley to turn around.

Nurse Maidenkirk was nearly unrecognizable in a sleek black pantsuit. Next to her, dressed in his usual pin-striped double-breasted suit, was Hammett.

"Wouldn't it be easier to text us when you want to meet instead of constantly popping up?" Shelley wondered aloud.

"Text messages are a dangerous game. They're easier to hack into than a box of mac and cheese. Now, follow me, kiddos," Hammett said, leading them to a quiet corner, away from the hustle and bustle of the station.

After catching Hammett and Nurse Maidenkirk

up on the latest developments, Jonathan and Shelley relaxed. There was something comforting about Hammett, almost parental. They could rely on him, they could trust him, and right now they couldn't say that about anyone else. Not in England, anyway.

"Go back to the origin of the environmentalist story," Hammett said, pulling a toothpick from his mouth. "Who told you Nina was an environmentalist?"

"Prime Minister Falcon," Shelley answered.

"And who told the prime minister?"

"Randolph," Jonathan replied.

"And who told Randolph?"

"Darwin, Oli, and Hattie," Jonathan responded.

"So someone misunderstood?" Hammett proposed.

"These aren't the type of people to misunderstand," Jonathan pointed out. "They're annoyingly detail oriented."

"It's true. They're even worse than Jonathan," Shelley added.

"So maybe there's more to this case than meets the eye," Hammett declared as he popped the toothpick back into his mouth. "You need to find out.

And fast. LIQ-30 is one scary virus, especially for your lot. Average, unexceptional kids can't afford to lose focus or intelligence. Bottom line, you don't have enough to spare."

"What a long and interesting history we've had with viruses," Nurse Maidenkirk mused. "Did you know the Spanish flu killed fifty million people?"

"No, I didn't," Jonathan answered flatly.

"Did you know that smallpox killed three hundred million people up through the twentieth century?"

"Nope," Shelley responded. "And to be honest, I could have easily gone the rest of my life without knowing those facts."

"Listen here, kiddos," Hammett said as he placed a hand on both Jonathan's and Shelley's shoulder. "The nobodies of this world are counting on you. Don't let them down."

OCTOBER 24, 6:01 P.M. RESTAURANT. LONDON, ENGLAND

After talking to Hammett, Jonathan and Shelley realized that the only surefire way to get to the bottom of things was to spy on the spies, i.e., Oli, Hattie, and Darwin. And though Jonathan and

Shelley were not even fractionally as well versed in espionage as the BAE agents, their forgettable nature made trailing targets a cinch.

"What are you thinking?" Jonathan asked Shelley as they peered into the restaurant's main dining room, where Oli, Hattie, and Darwin were seated.

"The coat closet," Shelley said as she motioned toward a nearby door. "We'll be out of the way and yet still able to keep an eye on them."

"Good thinking," Jonathan responded as the two slipped into the closet.

Crouched on the floor, peering out from behind the coats, Shelley whispered, "I don't mean to be a pain, but I feel like spotting this location was more than *good* thinking, it was *great* thinking."

"You know what I like about you, Shells?"

"Everything."

"You're not afraid to give yourself a compliment," Jonathan said.

"What choice do I have? I'm an unexceptional. Who else is going to compliment me?" Shelley said as she watched a waiter approach Darwin, Oli, and Hattie's table with a basket of bread and a bottle of olive oil.

Jonathan gasped. "Did you see that?"

"Of course I did!" Shelley replied. "But just in case I missed it, why don't you tell me anyway?"

"Hattie laughed at the same time as Darwin when Oli finished speaking—she understood a joke. How could she understand a joke that quickly? Post-contamination, she's averaging a two- to three-minute lag time for anything more complicated than a knock-knock joke, and that's if she can concentrate long enough to even listen to the joke!"

"Maybe Hattie's future laughing," Shelley suggested.

"That's not a real thing. We made it up to explain why you were laughing when you didn't know who Neville Chamberlain was!"

Shelley nodded. "Oh yeah, that's right."

Jonathan suddenly grabbed hold of Shelley's shoulder. "What if Hattie wasn't contaminated with LIQ-30 at all? What if she's faking it?"

"Johno, you know I love jumping to a conclusion more than just about anyone. It's actually listed on my résumé as a hobby. Okay, that part's not true, but you get the idea. My point is, so she laughed; is that really enough to say she's faking LIQ-30 contamination? She might have been laughing at a joke

Oli told five minutes earlier for all we know. Since we can't hear them, it's hard to say anything for sure."

"You're right."

Shelley smiled. "Those three words never get old, do they?"

"It's actually only two words because *you're* is a contraction."

"Enough with your details!"

"Don't you mean meat tails?"

"They're on the move," Shelley noted as Oli, Darwin, and Hattie walked away from the table.

Jonathan and Shelley dashed out of the restaurant just as the trio stepped into a taxi.

"Come on," Shelley said as she pulled Jonathan toward a waiting black cab.

"But we don't have any money!"

"So we'll give the driver an IOU!"

"No one accepts IOUs in the real world!" Jonathan cried. "I don't even accept them in Monopoly!"

"Oh, forget it!" Shelley groaned as the taxi carrying the BAE agents pulled away. "It's too late. They're gone."

OCTOBER 24, 8:00 P.M. 10 DOWNING STREET. LONDON, ENGLAND

Seated at the kitchen table, Mrs. Cadogan smiled kindly at Jonathan and Shelley as she scooped large helpings of stew onto their plates. "I gave Piper the cat a taste of the meat an hour ago. Poison usually takes effect in less than sixty minutes."

"And Piper's still alive?" Shelley asked.

"She most certainly is," Mrs. Cadogan confirmed as she squeezed her plump frame into a chair and then quickly shoveled a large spoonful of food into her mouth.

After swallowing his first bite, Jonathan looked at Mrs. Cadogan and smiled. "This is really delicious."

"Thank you," Mrs. Cadogan said. "Now then, children, did you think of any more questions?"

"Questions?" Shelley repeated.

"You've had so many questions lately."

"We have?" Jonathan replied.

"Popping up at all hours to question me. In my time, children were taught to respect their elders! Not interrogate them!" Mrs. Cadogan said before abruptly pausing to look around the room. "Is anyone hiding in the cupboards?"

Jonathan shook his head. "No, Mrs. Cadogan, they're not."

"If you find anyone hiding in the cupboards, you mustn't trust them, children! They're not who you think they are."

"I once spent three hours locked in a cupboard," Shelley said, closing her eyes as if to recall the memory. "My sister thought I deserved jail time for cutting the heads off her dolls."

Jonathan released a long sigh, shook his head, and then asked, "Why, Shells? Why?"

"The dolls had a superiority complex. They thought they were better than me, but I showed them, didn't I?"

"They're coming," Mrs. Cadogan said ominously. "They're coming for you. Tonight."

"Good to know," Jonathan responded casually. "Could you pass the salt?"

OCTOBER 25, 1:02 A.M. 10 DOWNING STREET. LONDON, ENGLAND

Jonathan sat straight up in bed, sickness rising in his throat. He was shivering, nauseated, and weak. An unfamiliar feeling took hold, one that Jonathan had rarely if ever experienced—homesickness. Never mind that his mother and father's idea of nursing him back to health usually involved copious amounts of candy bars, soda, and video games. In that moment, Jonathan felt so sick that he actually missed his parents.

Slumped against the doorway, Shelley moaned, "I don't feel so good."

"Neither do I," Jonathan groaned.

"They've poisoned you!" Mrs. Cadogan hollered from behind Shelley.

Jonathan turned his head to look at the old woman. "Are you and Piper okay?"

"We're fine," Mrs. Cadogan answered, holding the cat in her arms.

"How is that possible? We ate the same things," Shelley said.

"No! The cake. Our *favorite* cake!" Jonathan said in between moans.

"The carrot cake!" Shelley realized as she dropped to the floor, too weak to stand.

"Did you make the carrot cake yourself?" Jonathan asked Mrs. Cadogan as he pulled himself from his bed in an attempt to help Shelley.

"No, of course not! We're in the middle of a war! I haven't the rations to make such things!" Mrs. Cadogan answered, referring to the public's limited access to foods such as sugar and flour during the Second World War.

"Then where did the cake come from?" Shelley asked, sprawled out on the floor.

"The cake was delivered this afternoon, addressed to the two of you," Mrs. Cadogan explained.

"Do you still have the box?" Jonathan asked, his face now pale green.

"I never throw away boxes from Petit Four and Petit More bakery. They're far too pretty," Mrs. Cadogan said as Jonathan pushed past her and made a mad dash for the bathroom.

Shelley scowled and then weakly banged her fist against the floor. "Nina's favorite bakery."

OCTOBER 25, 8:01 A.M. BAE HEADQUARTERS.
LONDON, ENGLAND

After emptying their bodies of every morsel of carrot cake they had eaten and then sleeping a few hours, Jonathan and Shelley summoned the energy to drag themselves to BAE headquarters to meet with Randolph, Darwin, Oli, and Hattie.

"Nina's warning you to back off," Darwin said upon hearing of the special delivery Jonathan and Shelley received the night before. "Next time she might try something even more drastic."

"More drastic than trying to drown us in a medieval pit and poisoning our food?" Shelley said with a scoff. "Is that even possible?"

Darwin raised his eyebrows and then motioned toward Hattie, who was staring at the screen saver on the computer.

"What a glorious day!" Hattie remarked. "We really must go outside. Just look at how the sun is shimmering on the water."

A light tremor worked its way up Jonathan's body, from his toes to his legs, then his stomach and chest. His lungs tightened; his breathing grew labored. Fear, pure and simple, was taking hold. Jonathan was petrified of losing the minimal intelligence he had. As it was, he was just barely making it through life. What would happen if his intelligence decreased, if he grew even more confused? He would have no choice but to depend on his parents. And as Jonathan learned as a toddler when his parents forgot him in the frozen foods section at 7-Eleven, his mother and father were nice people, but they were not to be relied upon.

"Jonathan? You're looking a bit peaked," Oli said, his brow furrowed with concern.

"Depending on what Nina used to poison you, it's possible you still have traces in your system, which could make you sick," Darwin said as he placed a glass of water in front of Jonathan.

"No need to worry, turning green is just one of Jonathan's many party tricks," Shelley said as she pulled him out of his seat and whispered in his ear, "Get it together, we're spies. We can't turn green at every mention of intellectual annihilation!"

"You always did have a way with words," Jonathan said before turning to the others. "I think I'll get some air."

Seconds after Jonathan left, Shelley stood up and announced, "I should probably go with him just in case he gets hit by a bus and someone needs to identify the body."

OCTOBER 25, 8:26 A.M. STREET. LONDON, ENGLAND

"So you didn't find anything conclusive after trailing Hattie, Oli, and Darwin?" Hammett asked, huddled in the corner of a nearby square with Jonathan, Shelley, and Nurse Maidenkirk.

"Only that Hattie seemed to laugh at Oli's comment, but since we couldn't actually hear what was said, we can't say for sure," Jonathan responded.

"However, we can say for sure that we were

poisoned by a cake sent to us from Nina's go-to bakery," Shelley said before pausing to rub her chin. "The only thing I can't figure out is how she knew carrot cake was our favorite."

"Maybe it was just a lucky guess?" Jonathan suggested, and then shuddered. "I don't know what she put in that cake, but I have never been so sick in my life."

"Espionage and poison go together like peanut butter and jelly," Nurse Maidenkirk piped up. "Did you know that polonium-210 was used to kill an operative right here in London not so long ago? But operatives always have been rather imaginative when it comes to death. Death by poison. Death by allergy. Death by stairs. Death by drowning. Death by—"

"We get the idea," Hammett interrupted Nurse Maidenkirk before turning his attention to Jonathan and Shelley. "I know you're scared, because darn it, who wouldn't be? You're facing a tough broad. A mean broad. A ruthless broad. Someone willing to do just about anything to get you off her tail."

Shelley pushed her messy blond hair out of her face and nodded. "That's what we're afraid of."

"If Nina infects us with LIQ-30, we don't think

our parents are equipped to handle it," Jonathan admitted.

"Don't worry, kid. We take care of our own; on that you have my word," Hammett stated stoically. "And if you two just want to hit the road, get out of Dodge, I'd understand that too."

"You mean quit?" Shelley asked.

"Yes. Take a breather from this whole espionage game," Hammett said. "It's not for everyone."

"We're not everyone," Shelley said before pausing. "Or, actually, we kind of are."

Jonathan shook his head. "We're not quitting. Not now. Not ever. This is all we have in life. And we're not walking away from it, no matter how dangerous."

"There it is again," Shelley said, raising her hand for a high five. "The reason this guy's my hero eight percent of the time."

"You said eleven percent a couple days ago," Jonathan interjected.

"I did? Don't take it personally. Numbers have never been my thing."

"You two look awfully tired," Nurse Maidenkirk said, examining Jonathan's and Shelley's faces.

"Not to worry, though. I just so happen to have a vitamin shot ready," she continued, pulling an impressively long needle from the front pocket of her dress.

"Leave them alone, Maidenkirk! They've got enough problems as it is," Hammett said, and then popped a new toothpick into his mouth.

"We should get back to headquarters," Jonathan said as he looked at his watch. "The others are going to start to wonder what happened to us."

"I believe in you two. If I didn't, I'd pull you from the field, right here, right now," Hammett said. "But I'm not the one on the front lines. I'm not the one with a target on my back."

"No," Jonathan replied. "That's us."

"If life has so much to offer, then
why do I have so little?"

—Gavin Kertzner, 10, Toronto, Canada

CHAPTER 12

<221274-GZ-LOUC-369>

OCTOBER 25, 9:18 A.M. STREET. LONDON, ENGLAND

"I've spent most of my life wanting to be someone else. Anyone else. I've even imagined climbing into someone else's body, and feeling better with their face, their voice, their brain, their everything," Jonathan said as he walked back to BAE headquarters with Shelley.

"That's some pretty creepy science fiction stuff," Shelley said, raising her eyebrows. "But I know what you mean. Until League, I never had a real reason to feel good about myself."

"We aren't going to turn our backs on the mission, are we?" Jonathan asked.

"No way," Shelley said as she placed her arm around Jonathan's shoulders. "We've got each other. Nothing can stop us. Except of course for a tsunami or a coma or jail—"

"Shells," Jonathan interrupted. "Even though you're technically my first and only friend, you're also my best friend."

"Can I get that in writing?" Shelley asked, and then paused to think. "On second thought, why don't you just send me an e-mail at your earliest convenience. That way I can forward it to the necessary people. Seriously, though, no rush. But if I could get it by the end of the week, that would be great."

"As long as I can still figure out how to turn on a computer when this mission ends, you'll have my e-mail."

"Oh, and Johno? You're my best friend too. Eighty-four percent of the time, anyway."

"Eighty-four," Jonathan said with a smile. "I'll take it."

Buzz. Buzz. Buzz.

"It's probably Darwin and Oli wondering where we are," Jonathan said as he pulled his phone from his pocket and opened his text messages.

> **UNKNOWN NUMBER:** Leave now or you're next. No more warnings.

OCTOBER 25, 10:02 A.M. BAE HEADQUARTERS. LONDON, ENGLAND

"Welcome back. Feeling better?" Darwin asked Jonathan and Shelley while seated at a table with Oli and Hattie.

"Nina's threatening to infect us!" Shelley blurted out, and then paused, realizing how hysterical she sounded. "Just kidding. That was my imitation of how a frightened, inexperienced operative might react."

"I don't understand," Oli said calmly while drinking a cup of tea. "What happened?"

"We just received an anonymous text. It says, 'Leave now or you're next. No more warnings,'" Jonathan read aloud from his phone.

"Nina's coming for you," Darwin announced. "She knows you're on her trail. And she doesn't want to take any chances."

"With all due respect, you're out of your league. Nina's a first-class operative. You simply don't stand a chance against her," Oli stated unequivocally as he placed his teacup on the table.

Jonathan stared at Oli intensely, so intensely that a vein on his forehead started to throb. He had spent his whole life, all twelve years of it, telling himself that he couldn't do things. And now that he finally felt strong enough to face the world, he wasn't going to let some tea-sipping academic tell him he couldn't! Never mind that a mere hour ago the boy was on the verge of fainting from fear. That was then. And this is now.

"We can handle it," Jonathan responded firmly.

"You sure about that?" Darwin asked, looking over at Hattie, whose lips were moving as she read. "Because if you want out, we understand."

"We're not quitting," Shelley asserted. "Not now. Not ever."

"To risk your minds for a country that isn't even your own, are you sure you want to do that?" Darwin pressed on.

"We're sure," replied Jonathan. "Aren't we, Shells?"

"As sure as Randolph has one eye."

Jonathan sighed. "A simple yes would have done it."

OCTOBER 25, 2:00 P.M. BAE CAFETERIA. LONDON, ENGLAND

Tense and on edge, Jonathan and Shelley pushed their trays along the counter, stopping to pile food on their plates every few seconds.

"Shells," Jonathan said, wiping his forehead with his hand. "I'm sweating. A lot. Not a normal

amount. An amount that feels dangerous. Maybe we got carried away back there? Maybe we should have taken the out?"

"Did you see Hattie moving her lips as she read?" Shelley asked, nervously fidgeting with an apple. "It took me years to stop doing that. You don't know the shame. In my family, a family of geniuses, to move your lips while reading?! It was unheard of! I used to smuggle menus into the bathroom at restaurants just so I could read them in peace."

"You could have just covered your mouth with your hand," Jonathan said as he placed a carton of milk on his tray.

"That's even weirder than moving your lips while you read!" Shelley scoffed. "You have the worst ideas."

"Look who's talking! Aren't you the girl who wants to use giraffes as cell towers?"

"Giraffes are way better looking than those ugly metal things."

"You need help," Jonathan whispered through gritted teeth.

"You're right, I do need help. I need a partner who can actually tell time," Shelley snapped.

"I've never had a problem telling time, at least not recently," Jonathan responded. "And FYI it's *library*, not *liberry*!"

"I know that!"

"You sure about that?" Jonathan asked, raising his eyebrows.

"As sure as the sky is blue, which is most of the time, but not all of the time because of clouds and rainy days and stuff," Shelley rambled as she fiddled with her glasses.

"Can't you ever just answer a question with a simple yes or no?" Jonathan said with a huff.

"Yes," Shelley said, and then pursed her lips as though trying to hold back the words. "See? I just did it!"

Jonathan didn't respond; he simply stared at Shelley. She was the only person in the world whom he truly trusted. Not just in London. Or the United Kingdom. Or even in the United States. But the whole world. And it wasn't just because she knew his name, both first and last, but because she knew *him*, she understood him. And that was something that even Jonathan's own parents couldn't say.

"Johno," Shelley said. "You've been staring at

me for a really long time. And frankly, you're starting to remind me of this cat I once knew who had rabies. He used to sit in the corner and glare at people. It was really creepy. And not just because he was foaming at the mouth."

"Shells, I don't want to fight with you," Jonathan admitted. "We can fight with the whole world if we need to, but let's not fight with each other."

"No problemo," Shelley said, removing her glasses and smiling at him. "That means 'no problem' in Spanish."

"Got it," Jonathan said, nodding. "So we had a little freak-out. We let our nerves get the better of us, but we're still going to do this. We're going to stop Nina, right?"

"Right," Shelley confirmed.

"So how are we going to find her?" Jonathan asked.

"According to the text message, Nina's going to find us."

"I think it's worth risking our brains, the little we have, anyway, for someone else's country," Jonathan said as much for himself as for Shelley.

"Of course it is! Why should a person's birth-place be a reason not to help them?"

Jonathan stared at Shelley, so impressed by her statement that he was actually a little stunned.

"Are you okay?" Shelley asked, grabbing hold of Jonathan's arms. "You look like you have serious indigestion."

"I do? That was my 'I'm proud of you' look."

"You definitely need to work on it, then."

"I still remember the day my grandmother told me I was smart. I cried. I couldn't believe my parents had left me in the care of someone so foolish."

—Decca Sherak, 13, Colorado City, Colorado

CHAPTER 13

<834097-DS-LOUC-194>

OCTOBER 26, 6:42 A.M. 10 DOWNING STREET. LONDON, ENGLAND

Jonathan slept, as he always did, on his back with his arms by his sides and his legs straight. It was a position he assumed nightly when he crawled into bed and, except for the odd bout of the flu, he never deviated from this pose. For at his core, Jonathan believed that people like his parents who stretched out in bed, flip-flopping around like a fish pulled from the sea, were expending unnecessary energy.

The sound of something crashing through

Jonathan's window prompted him to sit straight up in bed and scream, "Shelley!"

And though Shelley was responsible for loud noises near him 99 percent of the time, this time she wasn't.

"Johno! Johno!" Shelley called out groggily after throwing open the door to his room. "Who's dead? Please don't say us, because if this is heaven, I want a refund."

"Shells, I have to tell you something, but before I do, I need you to promise me that you're going to stay calm. Okay?"

"How can I promise if I don't know what you're going to say? Why don't you tell me and then I'll let you know if I can make that promise?"

"No, Shells! You need to promise!"

"Fine! I promise! Just stop dragging this out, Johno!"

Jonathan then took a deep breath and held up a jalapeño tied to a rock. "Look what just came through the window."

Shelley nodded. She rubbed her chin. She furrowed her brow. And finally she spoke.

"Don't kill me, but what do jalapeños mean again?"

"It means there's an emergency! We could be in danger! We need to find Hammett!"

"More danger? How could we possibly be in *more* danger?" Shelley asked, theatrically throwing her hands up in the air.

"I don't know. The jalapeño lets us know there's an emergency; it doesn't give specifics," Jonathan explained as he started for the bathroom. "We need to get dressed and hit the street as soon as possible. Okay?"

"Okay."

"You can do this; I've got your back," Jonathan whispered to himself in the bathroom mirror. "Sure, you're scared. Sure, you lack muscles and any real upper-body strength. Sure, you're facing down someone with actual espionage training." The boy then dropped his head and sighed. "This must be the worst pep talk in the history of pep talks."

While shaking his head at himself in the mirror, Jonathan heard the sound of someone crying and gasping for air. And it wasn't just anyone, he realized—it was Shelley. After racing back into his bedroom, Jonathan discovered Shelley huddled in a ball on the floor of his room—red-faced, covered in sweat, and foaming at the mouth. Jonathan was sure that she was dying. Or that she had rabies.

Assuming the role of paramedic, Jonathan checked Shelley's vitals, noting that her pupils were not dilated and that her heartbeat, while elevated, was nothing out of the ordinary.

"Eh...duh...duh..." Shelley mumbled incoherently.

"I don't understand," Jonathan said, pulling out his cell phone. "I'm calling an ambulance!"

Shelley grabbed for the phone, but Jonathan was quicker.

"Don't...call..."

"I'm not going to sit here and watch my only friend die!" Jonathan screeched as he dialed 911. Only it didn't ring. Instead he heard a strange sound and an automated voice telling him that he had dialed an incorrect number.

"What?" Jonathan screamed, in full panic mode. "Nine-one-one doesn't work in England!"

"Dumb," Shelley finally muttered.

"You're going to use your last breaths to insult me?"

"*I* d-did something d-dumb. I ate the jalapeño," Shelley stammered.

"You ate the jalapeño? Why would you do that?" Jonathan blustered.

"I wanted to impress you."

"Shells," Jonathan said, grabbing her hand. "Why would you ever think that would impress me?"

"I don't remember. The tornado of fire in my mouth and lower intestines caused my hard drive to crash," Shelley said, fanning herself with a magazine.

"Never eat the messages, Shells," Jonathan said before muttering under his breath, "If you had read *How to Make Great Popcorn in the Microwave*, you would know that."

Jonathan and Shelley passed through the gate in front of 10 Downing Street and turned left. And though they had not yet caught sight of Hammett or Nurse Maidenkirk, having just received the jalapeño, Jonathan and Shelley knew they were close by.

"Turn right," Shelley whispered to Jonathan. "You'll see a garden square with lots and lots of trees. It's as good a cover as we're going to get in broad daylight."

Jonathan and Shelley had only just taken a seat on a secluded bench, hidden from the street by two large shrubs and a low-hanging tree, when Hammett and Nurse Maidenkirk arrived dressed as street cleaners.

"Sit down, kiddos, and listen. I mean really listen," Hammett said before pausing to look around. "We've got news. Big news. The kind of news that could blow your socks off, if you know what I mean."

"A great many people die while trying to put their socks on," Nurse Maidenkirk added.

"Last night, we were down by the wharf, something to do with a bird that exploded after eating uncooked rice," Hammett said, shaking his head. "A gruesome, gruesome scene."

Nurse Maidenkirk nodded. "Intestines everywhere."

Hammett waved his hand for Nurse Maidenkirk to stop talking. "Then *she* appeared."

"The ghost of the dead bird?" Shelley gasped.

"What I've got to tell you is important, real important, kiddo. So what do you say you do more listening and less talking? Get it? Got it? Good!" Hammett barked, then popped a toothpick into his mouth. "Like I was saying, we were walking along the wharf and the next thing I knew, Nina appeared."

"Nina?" Jonathan repeated.

"That's right, Nina," Hammett responded. "There she was, no more than three feet from us. I was staring at the girl, wondering what I should do, when she dropped a letter and took off running."

"I picked up the letter while Hammett tried to catch her," Nurse Maidenkirk said.

"But she lost me," Hammett said, lowering his head, clearly a little embarrassed.

"And the letter?" Jonathan asked.

Hammett nodded and then pulled a small white envelope from his pocket.

"It's addressed to us," Shelley noted quietly as Hammett unfolded a piece of paper on which was written: *You're wrong. Meet me at the London Eye at 8:00 p.m.*

"Who does she think she is, telling us that we're wrong?" Shelley said with a huff.

"Calm down, Shells. We don't even know what she's talking about."

"Exactly," Shelley said. "Would it have killed her to be a little more specific? We're spies, not mind readers."

Pushing his black locks away from his forehead, Jonathan quietly uttered, "We need to go, we need to try and talk some sense into Nina."

"You mustn't forget that she's already tried to kill you a couple of times," Nurse Maidenkirk reminded Jonathan. "And as the saying goes, the third time's a charm."

"My gut says it's a trick and my gut's never

wrong, except about roller coasters. It always says to go on them, and it never turns out well," Shelley admitted.

"But what if it's not a trick? Or even if it is, it's still an opportunity to catch Nina," Jonathan pointed out.

"That's true," Shelley conceded.

"It's dangerous—" Hammett started to say when Shelley interrupted.

"I'm not afraid of danger! I just prefer the kind of danger where nothing happens to me."

"I understand," Jonathan said, nodding. "You love non-dangerous danger, the kind that always works out in the end."

"Exactly!" Shelley answered enthusiastically. "Finally, someone who gets me!"

OCTOBER 26, 9:08 A.M. 10 DOWNING STREET. LONDON, ENGLAND

After returning from their meeting, Shelley carefully hid Nina's note at the bottom of her dresser drawer, and then covered it with three T-shirts, a sweater, and a pair of socks.

"Until we figure out what's really going on, I say

we keep this note to ourselves," Jonathan said as Shelley closed the drawer.

"Agreed," Shelley said. "Let's keep this on a need-to-grow basis."

"Need to *know*, not need to grow. What would need to grow even mean?"

"It means that we only tell people who need the information to grow, to move forward in their lives."

Jonathan shook his head and sighed. "How did I wind up with you as my partner?"

"Mostly luck."

OCTOBER 26, 7:46 P.M. STREET. LONDON, ENGLAND

A chill had come to the city late in the after-noon. Familiar faces morphed into unfamiliar faces as they covered up with low-hanging hats and high-necked scarves. Blending, as they always did, into the crowd of tourists, Jonathan and Shelley approached the Eye.

"Personally, I've never been fond of Ferris wheels," Jonathan admitted. "Something about paying to be slowly thrust into the sky doesn't seem like a good deal."

"But the view!" Shelley responded excitedly.

"Good views are overrated. You can get that on a postcard."

"Dear Mr. Doom and Gloom, please stop raining on my parade! And by *parade*, I mean life!"

"First of all—"

"Again with that expression?"

"Ugh!" Jonathan moaned. "You really do know how to push my buttons."

"I'm not trying to, Johno. I just want you to realize how lucky you are to possibly be infected with LIQ-30 while visiting the Eye. Have you looked it up online? It isn't your average Ferris wheel. It's a state-of-the-art machine with private, enclosed pods that will give us amazing views of the city."

"Must you talk about being infected? It's hardly a confidence booster," Jonathan grumbled as he spotted the large white contraption in the distance.

"Being infected with a view is better than being infected without one. Trust me."

"If I'm going to be infected, I would prefer it

happen in a nice heated café with tea and cookies, not on some theme park attraction!"

Shelley stopped and looked at him. "It's not easy for you, is it?"

"What?" Jonathan asked.

"Life."

"You're just figuring that out now?"

Shelley smiled and slipped her arm through Jonathan's. "What do you say we turn that frown upside down?"

"I hardly think this situation warrants a smile."

"You might be right," Shelley admitted. "I'm thinking this might be more of an eye-patch-and-hook type of moment."

"You want me to dress like a pirate?"

"Pirates are scary. Almost as scary as clowns. Better yet, maybe you could be a clown-pirate hybrid? That would really freak Nina out!" Shelley said excitedly.

"No," Jonathan stated firmly. "I'm not losing the last few brain cells I have while in costume. Leave me with a little dignity, would you?"

"Stop hyperventilating. It's not like I have a costume tucked in my bag. I was just trying to take your mind off—"

"Our impending stupidity?"

"I was going to say the great unknown, but it's true that stupidity is a definite possibility."

Standing at the base of the Eye, Shelley and Jonathan both felt the muscles in their jaws constrict. What was going to happen? Would they be able to talk Nina out of her plan? And if not, would they be able to capture her without being infected? Tighter and tighter the muscles in their jaws grew, giving them both pounding headaches.

"Do you have an aspirin, Shells?"

"Do I seem like the kind of person who carries aspirin in her bag?"

"Not really."

"Well, you're right. But look what I do have!" Shelley said while unfolding a paper that said NINA in large black letters.

"You brought a sign?"

"So she knows who we are."

"Nina's been watching us," Jonathan responded. "She knows what we look like."

"We're unexceptionals, Johno. No one ever *really* remembers what we look like."

✳ ✳ ✳

Five minutes passed. Then ten. Then twenty. Cold, the wind whipping their sign about, Jonathan and Shelley huddled together for warmth.

"Talk about unprofessional. Nina's twenty minutes late!" Shelley grumbled.

"I know. It's the last ride of the night," Jonathan said as he pointed toward the Eye. "What do you say we do it?"

"But you hate Ferris wheels!"

"I know, but you don't. Plus, I think we should celebrate the fact that we're still moderately intelligent."

OCTOBER 26, 8:38 P.M. THE EYE. LONDON, ENGLAND

Alone in a pod, slowly moving away from the ground, Jonathan and Shelley stared out the window, their minds teeming with questions. What was their next move? How were they going to find Nina? Maybe they should loop in Darwin and Oli? Why hadn't Nina shown up?

As questions raced through Jonathan's and Shelley's minds, the lights in their pod began to buzz and flicker.

"Why do I feel like a man with a mask and a knife is about to appear?" Shelley said as she grabbed hold of Jonathan's arm.

"Because you've seen too many horror films," Jonathan replied. "It's just an electrical short, not that an electrical short can't turn into something dangerous like a fire."

Shelley squeezed Jonathan's hand as the lights buzzed even louder and flickered faster until finally shutting off completely. Standing in the pod, the only light coming from the city far below, Jonathan turned to Shelley.

"I don't want to scare you—"

"Has saying that ever stopped anyone from being scared?" Shelley responded as she silently rued the moment she stepped foot on this glorified Ferris wheel.

"Look at the other pods. We're the only one that's lost power," Jonathan pointed out. "Maybe it's just a coincidence."

"I don't believe in coincidences. And neither should you."

"Then we have a problem," Jonathan replied.

Thump. Clack. Clack.

Someone or something was on the roof of their pod.

"Maybe it's a bird," Jonathan suggested.

Shelley rolled her eyes. "Maybe it's a plane. Maybe it's Superman!"

The sound of drilling echoed through the pod.

"Does Superman have a tool belt?" Jonathan mumbled as his chest constricted and panic took hold.

Creak. Snap. Crack. And just like that, a petite teenage girl dressed in head-to-toe black climbed down into the pod.

"At last we meet," Nina said softly before breaking into an awkward smile.

Shelley pointed at the roof of the pod. "That was some entrance."

"Wouldn't it have been easier to meet in a café?" Jonathan asked.

"Oh, come on, you're operatives. Where's your sense of excitement?" Nina said as she stepped toward them. "Plus, you're being followed by Oli, Darwin, and Hattie, who are currently two pods behind us."

"They followed us here?" Jonathan repeated.

"Actually, they arrived before you, which tells me they already knew where you were going," Nina explained.

"That's impossible. We didn't tell anyone," Shelley said.

"She's telling the truth," Jonathan seconded

before furrowing his brow. Something wasn't right. Something he couldn't quite put his finger on.

"Nina, you seem like a smart girl," Shelley started. "Well, except for the whole climbing-through-the-roof-of-the-Ferris-wheel thing. That was really dumb. You could have easily fallen off."

As Shelley rambled, Jonathan continued to stare at Nina. What was it, the boy thought. What was it about her appearance that was gnawing at him?

"Anyway, like I was saying, you seem like a smart girl. I'm sure if we just sit down and talk, we'll come up with a million better ways to help the environment than poisoning those ministers with LIQ-30."

"You've got it all wrong," Nina began, when Jonathan suddenly gasped.

"That's it!" Jonathan screeched. "She's too short!"

"Please excuse my partner, he's having some kind of mental breakdown. No doubt the result of all our near-death experiences, thanks to you," Shelley said as she lowered her glasses to glare at Nina.

"No, Shells! That's just it! It couldn't have been

Nina who tried to kill us at the Tower of London. She's too short. If she had pushed us into the pit, we would have felt her hands on our backs, but we didn't. We felt them on the tops of our shoulders!"

"It's true," Nina said as she stepped closer to Jonathan and Shelley. "I've never tried to kill you. I've never even tried to hurt you. Why would I? Don't you see, we're on the same side!"

"How's that?" Shelley asked.

"We're trying to stop LIQ-30 from being used in the name of vigilante justice," Nina explained.

"But you're the one doing that," Shelley continued.

"No, I'm not. That's just some cover story Darwin, Oli, and Hattie came up with to distract you from what they're planning."

"Which is?" Jonathan asked.

"They want to use LIQ-30 to neutralize dangerous people before they are able to commit a crime," Nina explained. "The law requires proof in order to arrest someone. And the truth is, sometimes it's impossible to gather the evidence in time. And when that happens, people suffer."

"But to punish people, to take away their ability to focus and think clearly, before they've even done anything, doesn't seem right," Jonathan remarked.

"No, it doesn't, which is why I'm looking for a safe place to properly dispose of the virus," Nina said. "To make sure it never falls into the wrong hands."

Shelley ripped off her glasses and stomped her foot. "So Hattie wasn't contaminated? She's been pretending this whole time! Man, is she a good actress!"

"But we're not. And now we have to pretend like we don't know what Darwin, Oli, and Hattie are really up to," Jonathan grumbled. "That's not going to be easy."

"What are you talking about? You're operatives," Nina said. "Pretending is part of the job."

"Oh, yeah, right," Jonathan responded as he started to fidget with the zipper on his jacket.

"You seem awfully nervous for operatives," Nina said, narrowing her eyes at Jonathan and Shelley.

"Nervous? Us? No way!" Shelley shot back. "We're as cool as a couple of cucumbers in the produce aisle."

"No," Nina retorted. "You're not. You're anxious. You're unsure of yourselves."

"We are," Jonathan admitted. "And there's a good reason for that. We're members of the League of Unexceptional Children. A covert network that uses the United States' most average, normal, and utterly forgettable children as spies."

"Johno! We weren't supposed to tell anyone!"

"If we're going to help Nina, she needs to know the truth. She needs to know who she's dealing with," Jonathan explained.

"Thank you for trusting me," Nina said as she looked out the window. "We're almost down; I'd better go. I'll be in touch."

And just like that, the girl was gone.

OCTOBER 27, 8:23 A.M. BAE HEADQUARTERS. LONDON, ENGLAND

"You ready?" Jonathan asked Shelley as they prepared to enter BAE headquarters.

"It's going to be a piece of cake. Hattie's not the only actress in this crowd."

"Just do your best to stick to the plan and keep

the improvising to a minimum," Jonathan implored Shelley as he opened the door.

"Good morning, fellow operatives!" Shelley called out loudly upon seeing Randolph, Oli, Darwin, and Hattie seated at a table. "We come bearing news."

"Do tell," Randolph replied stiffly.

Shelley pulled out a chair, plopped down, and then blurted out, "Nina's fled to Castle Combe to see her grandmother."

"What did you say?" Darwin exploded, running his fingers through his hair.

"I said Nina's gone to Castle Combe to see her grandmother," Shelley reiterated.

Oli narrowed his eyes. "How on earth do you know this?"

"How on earth do I know this?" Shelley repeated as she pushed her messy blond locks out of her face. "Nina told me."

"You've spoken to Nina?" Darwin screeched as he stormed across the room, stopping inches from Shelley's face. "You spoke to Nina and you didn't tell us?"

"I spoke to Nina...in a dream. She said, '*Hey,*

girl, this is getting crazy so I am going to bolt, head on up to Granny's for some tea and biscuits, check ya later.' "

"That's how Nina speaks in your dreams?" Oli asked, clearly perplexed by the whole story.

"They're my dreams—she can speak any way she wants to, okay? I don't put rules on my guests," Shelley said with a huff.

"And by *guests*, she means people that randomly show up in her head while she's sleeping, not people she actually knows," Jonathan clarified.

"So the Castle Combe tip came from a dream?" Darwin clarified. "Hardly a reliable source."

"I get some of my best tips from dreams," Shelley pressed on. "If I were you, I would check it out."

"I don't think so," Darwin said, prompting Shelley to clench her jaw, disappointed that her plan to get the BAE agents out of town had failed.

"Jonathan? Shelley?" Randolph said while reading a message on his phone. "The prime minister's secretary has just written to inform me that you have guests waiting for you at Downing Street."

"Guests?" Jonathan asked.

"Your friends from America, Mr. Humphries and Ms. Maidenkirk," Randolph answered.

"Who are they?" Darwin asked.

"Our students," Shelley spat out quickly. "We tutor them in mahjong and backgammon—those are our specialties after all."

"You brought your students on a mission?" Oli asked as Jonathan sighed at Shelley's poorly thought-out cover.

"Of course not. They followed us," Shelley said. "To be honest, they're more stalkers than students. But they're old. So we don't have the heart to take out restraining orders."

"And on that note," Jonathan interjected, "I think it's time we attend to our stalkers and whatever backgammon or mahjong emergency they're dealing with today."

OCTOBER 27, 12:46 P.M. 10 DOWNING STREET. LONDON, ENGLAND

"Kiddos, there's trouble on the home front," Hammett announced to Jonathan and Shelley while pacing back and forth in the kitchen.

"But don't worry," Nurse Maidenkirk added. "No one's dead. Not yet, anyway."

"Thanks for those comforting words," Shelley said with a quick roll of the eyes.

"Would someone please tell me what's going on?" Jonathan demanded, his patience waning.

"It's nothing the nurse and I can't handle, but here's the thing: We're leaving this joint. We're kicking this pop stand. *Today.* And not because we want to but because we have to. All I can tell you is that when trouble calls, she means business."

"Why is trouble a girl?" Shelley asked, lowering her glasses and peering at Hammett.

Nurse Maidenkirk raised her eyebrows. "Shelley has a point."

"This conversation right here, right now, is exactly why trouble's a woman!" Hammett said.

"Sometimes it's best just to admit defeat and move on," Jonathan advised Hammett.

"You know, kid, you're not as dim a bulb as you seem."

"Thanks for the sort-of compliment," Jonathan responded.

"We spoke to the prime minister and one-eyed Randy this morning, gave them a quick rundown on the news. They're stiff and formal, but they're good eggs," Hammett said with a wink. "Keep your wits about you, kiddos. Trouble, whether it's a boy or a girl, is lurking all around you and don't you forget it."

OCTOBER 27, 2:46 P.M. HYDE PARK. LONDON, ENGLAND

"May I ask why you placed a jalapeño in my pocket?" Randolph said as he strolled through Hyde Park with Jonathan and Shelley.

"Shells, that's *League* code. Why would you expect Randolph to understand it?"

"I didn't, which is why I also placed a note in his pocket asking him to meet us in the park," Shelley explained.

"Then why did you put the jalapeño in there too?" Jonathan asked.

"An early Christmas gift."

"May we please get on with the matter at hand, whatever that may be?" Randolph interrupted.

"Randy? Can I call you Randy? And please feel free to call me Shelltastic."

"How kind of you," Randolph responded brusquely.

"He doesn't mean that, Shells, it's sarcasm," Jonathan explained.

"Luckily for you, I'm immune to sarcasm," Shelley said with a smile before her expression turned serious. "Here's the thing: We wanted to talk to you about Oli, Hattie, and Darwin. How well do you know them?"

"They were thoroughly vetted before joining BAE, so whatever you are implying or insinuating, I assure you, you are mistaken," Randolph stated curtly.

"Yeah, but you also thought Nina had been thoroughly vetted and now you think she's some kind of crazy radical," Shelley pointed out.

"I must admit the news about Nina was deeply shocking."

"Randolph, we don't have time to beat around the bush," Jonathan blurted out. "So I'm just going to come out and ask you whether it's possible that Darwin, Hattie, and Oli are trying to get their hands on LIQ-30 to use against possible threats to society."

"We also think they concocted the whole environmentalist story just to cover up the fact that Nina was actually trying to stop them," Shelley added. "Think about it. Did you ever know Nina to be an environmentalist before any of this happened?"

"Passions often hide below the surface, especially when espionage is involved. It is hardly unheard of for an operative to harbor secret political persuasions."

Frustrated, Shelley raised her voice. "Open your eyes, Randy! Can't you see that something is happening here?"

"Poor choice of words, Shells."

"I meant see with the one eye you have. Obviously you can't see with your glass eye," Shelley said before pausing. "And on that note, I would like to issue a formal retraction of everything I just said."

"You have nothing but tales. And in my world, facts are all that matter. Bring me proof and I will listen, but without it, you are not only wasting my time but your own. You need to focus on tracking Nina, not taking down your fellow operatives!" Randolph snapped before stomping away.

"That went well. And by *well*, I mean a total

disaster," Shelley said as she watched Randolph disappear from view. "I think it's time to go rogue."

"Meaning?"

"We wait for Nina's signal," Shelley answered. "And then we take them down."

OCTOBER 28, 6:22 A.M. 10 DOWNING STREET. LONDON, ENGLAND

"Wake up, Johno!" Shelley said, her face so close that he actually felt her breath warming his skin.

"Too comfortable, you are definitely too comfortable with me. A simple tap on the arm would have done the trick."

"It's time," Shelley announced.

"Time for what?"

"To get up and save the day."

"What?" Jonathan muttered, leaning forward in bed.

"Danger called and guess who answered? Me!"

"Shells, can you please stop talking like you're in a comic book and just tell me what's going on?"

"Nina texted. She finally found a safe laboratory to destroy LIQ-30."

"Excellent," Jonathan replied, stifling a yawn.

"Only, she needs our help breaking in."

"It's beginning to feel like breaking and entering is as normal as using a key," Jonathan moaned.

"I'm glad to hear you say that, because we're breaking into Buckingham Palace. You know, the queen's house, her crib, her main pad, her—"

And with that, Jonathan pulled the sheet over his head and sighed.

"Come on, Johno! Mrs. Cadogan's making breakfast. When I told her we were breaking into Buckingham Palace, she said we deserved pancakes!"

Pottering around the kitchen in a gray house-dress, a striped apron, and a gas mask sitting atop her head, Mrs. Cadogan appeared more than a little eccentric.

"Good morning, children," the old woman called out cheerfully as Jonathan and Shelley walked into the room.

"Someone woke up in a good mood," Jonathan noted as he took a seat at the table.

"Haven't you heard? We're winning the war!"

"Talk about old news," Shelley whispered to Jonathan as she grabbed a pancake. "Do you think

I should wear pearls? You know, just in case we run into Her Majesty."

"Shells, the queen has not invited us to tea. This is a mission, plain and simple. After that, it's back across the pond."

"...So, no pearls?"

OCTOBER 28, 2:03 P.M. BUCKINGHAM PAL-ACE. LONDON, ENGLAND

"Three children, please. And may I add, you really ought to consider expanding the age options. There needs to be something between child and adult; perhaps you could call it almost adult," Shelley suggested to the woman working the ticket booth at Buckingham Palace.

"I'm sorry, young lady, but did you say something?" the woman asked.

"Oh, I said something, all right!" Shelley replied with a huff as Jonathan pushed her out of the way.

"Three children, please," he repeated.

"That'll be sixty-two pounds, forty pence," the woman responded, handing over three tickets.

"Just think, Nina, soon the world will no longer be in danger of seriously confused people with

201

the attention span of gnats. Well, at least not newly confused people with the attention span of gnats," Shelley rambled as they waited for the start of the tour.

Nina looked around the ticket hall, anxiously checking for any sign of Hattie, Darwin, or Oli. "You're absolutely certain that they didn't follow you?"

"Following unexceptionals in a crowd isn't easy, even for BAE agents," Jonathan said.

"You're a lucky lot, you unexceptionals—natural-born operatives," Nina said with a faint smile.

"That's true, but it also means your dentist forgets who you are and removes a healthy tooth," Jonathan said as he touched his jaw, remembering the loss of a perfectly good molar.

Shelley rolled her eyes. "It only happened once. Don't be such a drama queen."

"It's taken quite a bit of work, but I've finally found a secure path to the laboratory," Nina leaned in and whispered to Jonathan and Shelley. "It's a relatively simple plan. But hopefully one that will work. You two are to break away from the tour upon entering the second stateroom. There will be a door in the southwest corner of the room—"

"Southwest?" Shelley repeated while rubbing her chin.

"I feel it's important you know that we have no sense of direction," Jonathan admitted to Nina.

"Can you tell your left from your right?" Nina asked with a furrowed brow.

"Most of the time," Shelley answered matter-of-factly.

"Very well, upon entering the second stateroom, there will be a door to your right. It leads to a staircase. Go to the second landing, climb out the window, shimmy across the roof until you see a storm drain, hold on to the pipe, and climb down to the balcony below, go through the window, and finally unlock the door. I will be on the other side. From there, we are a mere stone's throw from the laboratory."

"Are you sure you don't want to switch roles? You could do all the climbing and shimmying and then let us in?" Shelley asked.

"I'm afraid someone would see me. You two, on the other hand—"

"We know, we know, we're basically invisible," Jonathan interrupted.

"Are you sure you can handle this?" Nina asked.

"Can we handle this? Does the pope wear plaid?" Shelley scoffed.

"No, he doesn't," Nina responded. "He wears white."

"Really? How boring."

"What Shelley meant to say is, not only can we handle this, we're ready," Jonathan clarified.

"Ready like Freddie!" Shelley blurted out, and then winked at Nina.

"What are you talking about? Who's Freddie?"

"Nina, please forget that I even mentioned Freddie. And for the record, I don't know anyone named Freddie. Sometimes I just say things," Shelley explained. "Bottom line, I would like to issue a formal retraction of my statement regarding Freddie. So please forget that I even mentioned the boy's name. Or, at the very least, pretend like you've forgotten."

Nina's eyes started to prick with tears as she stared at Jonathan and Shelley. The mission was sure to fail with these two. There was simply no way around it. They had no idea what they were doing.

"You're worried we're going to let you down, aren't you? That we're going to sink the mission," Jonathan said as he grabbed hold of Nina's arm. "But here's the thing: There's no need to worry. We've never failed a mission yet."

Of course, there had only ever been one other mission, but Jonathan thought it best to send Nina off on a positive note.

"One hundred percent success rate," Shelley confirmed.

Nina's face relaxed. "I must admit that is a most impressive statistic."

"We know," Shelley said as the guide signaled that the next tour was starting.

OCTOBER 28, 2:24 P.M. BUCKINGHAM PALACE. LONDON, ENGLAND

Trailing behind the tour, Jonathan and Shelley were awestruck at the opulence of the palace. Crystal chandeliers dangled from thirty-foot ceilings. Intricate gold-leaf moldings lined the walls. And furniture that appeared straight out of a fairy tale covered the well-polished wooden floors.

"Is it just me, or does this whole vibe scream

Shelltastic?" Shelley asked as she took in the wonders of the first stateroom.

"Shelltastic likes chandeliers and thrones? Who knew?"

"Bottom line, I would love a castle."

"Well, I'll be sure to keep that in mind when your birthday rolls around," Jonathan responded as Shelley bent her knees and awkwardly bowed her head.

"I've been practicing my curtsy all morning, just in case the queen walks by."

"In the spirit of managing expectations, I feel you should know that the queen does not regularly, or ever, just pop up during tours of the palace," Jonathan explained as they entered the second stateroom.

"This is just another reason why you have the nickname Dream Killer!" Shelley said with a huff as Jonathan turned his attention to finding the door.

"Look to your right, Shells. That's it. That's the door."

Shelley nodded and then turned her head.

"No, Shells, your other right."

As the tour prepared to leave the second stateroom, Jonathan and Shelley did what they did best—they blended into the background. Standing between two marble statues, they exchanged glances. Was it possible the tour guide would spot them? After all, the security guard at the museum had noticed Shelley when she pulled the fire alarm. But as the minutes passed, they relaxed. And soon the tour was gone.

"Let's go," Jonathan whispered, and then rushed across the room.

"Is the theme song for *Mission: Impossible* playing in your head too?" Shelley asked, eyes twinkling with excitement.

"No, I'm too busy thinking about what English prisons are like," Jonathan replied, then flung open the door and sprinted up the stairs.

However, after nine steps, both Jonathan and Shelley were red in the face and totally out of breath.

"Maybe it's best we just walk quickly," Jonathan suggested in between gasps of air, leaning against the wall.

Unable to even speak, Shelley nodded in agreement.

"There's the window," Jonathan said as they reached the top of the stairs.

"Wait! We're supposed to crawl across that?"

Shelley said, looking out the window at the narrow sliver of roof, no more than six feet wide.

"You'll be fine," Jonathan reassured Shelley.

"Not if I roll off! There's nothing to break my fall but the cold hard ground!"

"Shells, we have a job to do. We can't let our fears take over."

"You're right," Shelley conceded as she followed Jonathan out the window.

"Just don't look down," he instructed as they started slowly slinking across the tiled roof. "Look at the view of London! Look at the sky! Look anywhere! Just don't look down!"

"Do you believe in ghosts?"

"Really, Shells? You want to talk about ghosts *now*?"

"I'm pretty sure a ghost has entered my body with the sole purpose of making me look down! There's no other explanation! It's like someone's pulling my eyes over to the ledge!"

"Don't do it, Shells!"

But the girl couldn't help it. Something deep within her needed to know if the drop-off was as scary as she imagined.

"Johno…Johno…Johno."

"Please stop saying my name; it's making me *very* nervous," Jonathan sputtered as everything from the soles of his feet to his scalp started sweating.

"It's a long way down, Johno," Shelley whispered. "A really long way down."

"Not helpful, Shells!"

" 'Two twelve-year-old children died today at Buckingham Palace after falling off the roof.' "

Jonathan clenched his jaw. "How is writing a press release about our deaths helping the situation?"

"All I can hope is that they spell *Shelley* correctly. You know, a lot of people don't put the extra *e* in. It's always been a point of pride for me, that my name is just the tiniest bit different."

"I know, Shells. But can we please stop talking about our deaths and focus on scaling down the drainpipe?"

"Scaling down the drainpipe? What does that mean?"

"It means we're going to hold on to the drainpipe and climb down the wall to the balcony a floor below."

"The balcony *way* down there?"

"That's the one," Jonathan responded.

"There is no way I'm doing that! Forget it! Let the Brits fend for themselves!"

"Shells, before you decide anything, what do you say we stop and take a deep breath?"

"I hate it when people say that!" Shelley griped. "I spend every second of my life breathing—why is breathing *a little deeper* so special? Is it a magical unicorn sent to solve all my problems? I don't think so!"

"I'm sorry, Shells. I never meant to imply that taking a deep breath was anything like a magical unicorn sent to solve all your problems," Jonathan said calmly. "I just wanted us to pause for a second and think. What's scarier—climbing down a drainpipe where there is a slight possibility that you will fall and break every bone in your body or letting Nina down, failing the mission, and allowing LIQ-30 to wind up in the wrong hands?"

"Breaking every bone in my body."

"Shelley Brown, do you really mean that?"

"Do not use my full name! This is not a court of law!"

"This is the moment. We either step up and risk our lives to be great, to be the people that Hammett thinks we are, or we roll over and fail. And this isn't like failing math or English. There's no summer school. There's no second chance."

Shelley took a deep breath. And then paused, having realized what she had done. "I have to admit, it does kind of help."

Jonathan smiled.

"I'm not ready to say good-bye to Shelley Brown, International Lady of Espionage."

"Then start crawling."

And so they did, one hand over the other until they reached the edge of the roof, where they were presented with the thin metal drainpipe running along the wall to the balcony below.

"Hold my hand," Jonathan instructed Shelley.

"Eww, it's all sweaty."

"I'm going to pretend you never said that," Jonathan grumbled, then closed his eyes. "We can do this. Even nonathletes can climb *down* poles."

"Right," Shelley said before adding, "This is going to be a piece of cake...or maybe even just a bite of cake...or—"

"I'm going to start down now, so feel free to stop talking whenever you want."

Jonathan turned around and slowly pushed his legs off the edge of the roof, then slid down until he could grab hold of the drainpipe.

"Why does the balcony suddenly look so far away?" Jonathan asked, his voice cracking.

"Probably because you're holding on to a flimsy metal pipe that hasn't been secured for someone of your weight."

"I can't hear you. I can't hear you," Jonathan repeated as he slowly inched his way down, his eyes tightly closed.

Seven minutes later, when Jonathan finally made it to the balcony, Shelley took off her glasses and began moving toward the edge. "If I'm going to fall, I'd rather not see where I'm going."

"You can do it, Shells," Jonathan called out from below.

"Johno? If I should fall, could you at least try and catch me?"

Jonathan crossed his fingers and lied, "Of course, Shells, anything for you."

Eight minutes and forty-three seconds later, Jonathan sighed as he watched Shelley's feet land safely on the balcony. "Come on, we don't want to keep Nina waiting."

Jonathan and Shelley crawled through a window, slipped across the room, and unlocked the door.

"Now what?" Shelley asked just as the knob turned.

"I must say, so far I'm very impressed," Nina whispered as she rushed into the room.

"I can't tell you how many times a day I hear that," Shelley replied. "Sometimes it's exhausting listening to all the compliments."

"Take it down a notch, Shells," Jonathan whispered. "There's still a long way to go."

"This way," Nina instructed as she led Jonathan and Shelley down a service stairwell to the basement. "We're almost there."

Jonathan trembled with excitement; the destruction of LIQ-30 was finally within their reach. And frankly, he couldn't wait. To be moderately clever with an attention span good enough to rival any number of domesticated animals no longer seemed like such a bad thing.

"We're so close, I can almost taste it," Shelley whispered as she imagined the satisfaction of out-smarting *three* exceptionals.

"And we're in," Nina said as she picked the lock on the door to the laboratory.

Three square metal contraptions, each approximately the size of a golf cart, dominated the room. The chemical incinerators, as they were known, contained a latch similar in appearance to a trash chute, through which one could place items for destruction.

"We made it," Nina whispered, her eyes glistening with tears of joy as she stepped over empty glass vessels strewn about the floor.

"You most certainly did!" a voice came from behind one of the incinerators.

"Darwin?!" Nina shouted as the boy came into view.

"How could you possibly know that we were coming here?" Shelley squawked.

"Your little friend told us," Oli answered as he and Hattie stepped out from behind another incinerator.

"What on earth are you talking about?" Nina asked.

"Not *your* little friend," Hattie clarified. "*Their* little friend. Although, to be frank, Mrs. Cadogan is hardly little."

"Mrs. Cadogan?" Shelley repeated. "She thinks it's 1944!"

Jonathan shook his head. "Unless, of course, we've got another great actress in our midst."

"Dear boy, no one is that good of an actress!" Hattie responded with a laugh. "It may come as a surprise to you, given that Mrs. Cadogan does in fact think it's 1944, but she's remarkably aware of what's happening around her. And lucky for us, one needs only to ask to find out."

"It's true," Oli confirmed. "She even does a bit of light snooping if you tell her Winston Churchill himself has asked her to do so."

"Manipulating an old woman?" Nina remarked. "Why am I not surprised?"

"You say that as if you think we're evil," Darwin said as he stepped closer to Nina. "You used to understand that the world needs people like us, people who work outside the law."

"Every day I read about another horrific crime that could have been stopped but wasn't because of the mountain of evidence required for law enforcement to take something seriously," Oli lamented.

"But with LIQ-30, we have a humane way to stop these madmen before they have a chance to destroy lives," Darwin added.

"That sounds a lot like playing God," Nina said quietly.

"You can call it whatever you'd like, but the fact is we're just trying to protect innocent people," Darwin continued.

"But without due process, what do we become?" Nina asked, and then answered, "A dictatorship, and that's not who we are."

"No matter how hard we work, we will never foil all the plans," Darwin said, his face imploring Nina to hand over the vial.

"Can't you see that if you use LIQ-30, you destroy what makes this country great—freedom?" Nina said as she stepped closer to the incinerator.

"Stop!" Darwin shouted authoritatively. "You once believed in this plan. How can you betray us when we're so close?"

"Nina's not betraying you," Jonathan said. "She's protecting you from yourselves. She's stopping you from making the greatest mistake of your lives."

"Mistake? Dear boy, don't you understand?" Hattie said, shaking her head. "We're trying to help people!"

"This isn't the way to do it," Jonathan responded.

"Come on, guys, what do you say we destroy the vial, grab the queen and some scones, and get crazy," Shelley said, in an attempt to lessen the mounting tension of the situation.

"I couldn't agree more. And to prove the point, I myself will throw the vial into the incinerator," Darwin said as he stepped closer to Nina, with Oli and Hattie right behind him.

"That's not necessary," Nina responded, backing away.

"This is getting a little National Geographic and not in a good way. More in a three-lions-are-about-to-slash-an-antelope-before-ripping-it-limb-from-limb kind of way," Shelley said as she stepped between the two groups.

"Shells," Jonathan called out. "I'm not sure that's the best place to stand."

"I'm not allowing these three to get any closer to Nina."

Jonathan shook his head. It wasn't her intention, but Shelley's bold move had left him feeling weak and embarrassed. Why hadn't he stepped into the line of fire with the same ease as Shelley? Was she simply braver, more courageous than Jonathan? Yes, he thought. But she was also less attached to reality. Bottom line, Shelley was a little crazy.

"Sheila, no one wants to hurt you," Oli said as he stepped closer. "But we will if necessary."

It was at this moment that something useful caught Jonathan's eye, prompting him to bend down.

"Hey, Bob!" Darwin barked. "What are you doing?"

"Just tying my shoe," Jonathan replied meekly.

After turning back toward Nina, Darwin continued, "The future of this country is on the line, and we can't allow you or Bob or Sheila to get in our way."

"I've had just about enough of Bob and Sheila!" Shelley huffed.

"Our names are Jonathan and Shelley. Not Glasses and Khaki, and definitely not Bob and Sheila," Jonathan announced to the room.

Shelley smiled. "Yet another reason why this guy's my hero forty-three percent of the time."

"We may look dumb. We may sound dumb. In fact, we may actually be a little dumb," Jonathan said as he raised his left hand in the air. "But we've been around the block, so to speak…and we've learned that if you want something done right, you best do it yourself."

Jonathan then opened his left hand, revealing a small vial.

"And the plot quickens," Shelley announced before pushing her glasses up the bridge of her nose.

"*Thickens*. And the plot *thickens*," Jonathan corrected Shelley.

"No, *quickens*. As in action is happening."

"Guys?" Nina called out. "Now is not the time."

"Finally, something we can agree on, dear girl," Hattie said to Nina as she turned and started toward Jonathan, removing her earrings, gloves, and headband along the way.

"Be careful, Johno! Hattie might be small, but she's vicious. Sort of like an angry Pomeranian!"

Hattie flung herself to the ground and side-swiped Jonathan's calves with her legs, bringing the boy crashing to the floor.

"You will thank us one day!" Darwin hollered as he attempted to pin Jonathan's arms to the ground while Oli focused on wrangling the boy's legs.

"Get off my partner, you animals!" Shelley shrieked as she lunged at Darwin's back.

"Hattie? Do me a favor and get rid of this squirrel, would you?" Darwin said as Shelley opened her mouth and then closed it tightly around Darwin's ear.

"Ahhhhh!!!" the boy screeched. "She bit me!"

"I got it!" Oli cried triumphantly as he stood, covered in perspiration, vial in hand.

"You three never stood a chance against us," Darwin said as he looked from Jonathan to Shelley to Nina.

"One day you'll thank us for creating a better, safer world," Hattie said as she slipped on her gloves, earrings, and headband.

"We are leading the world into the light, and if in doing that we must use a drop of night, then so be it," Oli stated dramatically before adding, "And for the record, that is not a quote, but the work of my own brilliant mind."

"Don't romanticize it! This is wrong, plain and simple!" Nina yelled from across the room.

"You were once one of our most trusted allies. Somewhere deep within you, I know you understand," Darwin said as he motioned to Hattie and Oli that it was time to leave.

"See you around," Jonathan said with a smile as he placed an arm across Shelley's shoulders.

Darwin stopped. "Something isn't right here."

"They look rather pleased with themselves, don't they? Reminds me a bit of a partridge who knows you're a bad shot," Hattie remarked.

Darwin held the vial up to the light. "This isn't LIQ-30, is it?"

"Honestly, I have no idea what it is. I saw it on the floor and thought, *Hey, that would make a perfect decoy.*"

"And clearly it did," Shelley added. "But the

thing I still can't get over is that three highly trained operatives could believe that Nina would trust *Johno* with the vial!"

Darwin turned to Nina, eyes wide. "Give it to me."

"Unfortunately, Darwin, I dropped it in the incinerator while you guys were busy pinning that poor boy to the floor."

The look of defeat is unique in each person, and yet instantly recognizable. A combination of regret, shame, and sadness. Darwin lowered his eyes to the floor, Hattie pursed her lips and then silently mouthed a prayer. And Oli, in true Oli fashion, racked his mind for the perfect quote.

"Does Teeth know about this?" Darwin asked quietly, his mind still struggling to come to terms with what had just happened.

"Not yet," Shelley replied. "But he will shortly."

"We were trying to help the world, and now it is us who are to be punished?" Darwin said, shaking his head.

Jonathan, who had been silent this whole time, chimed in, "Not if I can help it."

"Excuse me?" Shelley said, placing her hands on her hips.

"Their hearts were in the right place, it's just that their heads weren't," Jonathan explained. "They're not criminals. Not in my opinion, anyway."

"Thank you, Bob. I mean, Jonathan," Hattie mumbled.

"But what they tried to do—Jonathan, they're basically vigilantes!" Shelley said, shaking her head.

"Every day you and I try our best to be exceptional, Shells. And every day we fail. Can you really say that mixed in with our honest attempts there weren't a few misguided ideas?"

"Maybe a few," Shelley admitted.

Hattie turned to Darwin and Oli. "Boys, I believe it prudent that we present our case to Randolph as soon as possible."

Oli nodded in agreement before turning toward Jonathan and Shelley. "In the words of Humphrey Bogart, 'I think this is the beginning of a beautiful friendship.'"

Shelley shook her head. "That feels like a bit of a stretch on account of the near drowning and food poisoning incidents. However, lukewarm acquaintances is definitely a possibility."

* * *

In the following days, after much discussion, Randolph and the prime minister would come to an agreement regarding the fates of Oli, Darwin, and Hattie. While their actions were most egregious, the prime minister thought it best to avoid formal criminal charges. Not only were they young, they had risked their lives time and time again for their country. And though Darwin, Oli, and Hattie had gone astray, their intentions were always in the right place: bettering the world. However, Prime Minister Falcon could not simply ignore what had happened. And so, in a fate worse than jail, Oli, Hattie, and Darwin were stripped of their BAE status. For in the end, their actions were deemed too drastic to be righted by a simple "I'm sorry."

But fortunately, not all was lost for Darwin, Hattie, and Oli. Their dismissal from BAE freed them up to pursue other passions. For Hattie, it was the stage. As it turned out, pretending to be less intelligent and less focused had sparked a genuine interest in acting. Darwin, on the other hand, was finally able to join the extracurricular club informally known as We Blow Things Up for Fun. And as for Oli, he delighted in discovering other history buffs capable of appreciating his vast repertoire of quotes.

And though each found happiness in their own way, they also took with them a nagging little voice that popped up every now and then and asked, *What could have been had you remained with the BAE?*

OCTOBER 29, 7:15 P.M. 10 DOWNING STREET. LONDON, ENGLAND

Seated at a long wooden table, a candelabra on each end, Prime Minister Falcon watched Jonathan and Shelley closely, still unsure what to make of the two of them.

"Randolph informed me of your great disappointment in missing the queen while at Buckingham Palace," the prime minister said while carefully cutting the vegetables on his plate.

"Meeting a member of the royal family has long been on my to-do list," Shelley said.

"But just so you know, pretty much everything is on her to-do list. And I do mean everything—learning the ukulele, space travel, hosting a television show in Bulgaria—"

"You are a most surprising set of assets," Prime Minister Falcon interrupted. "Barely intelligent enough to name all fifty states in the union, and yet you were able to find the truth in a very complicated situation. But perhaps most astounding, you acted on your beliefs, even when you lacked support from Randolph."

Jonathan smiled. "We're unexceptionals, sir. We're used to going through life without support."

"Without support? You've got me!" Shelley said before turning to the prime minister. "He calls me his rock."

Jonathan sighed. "I've never called you any such thing."

"Just to clarify, when I say *calls*, I don't mean with words, but with feelings," Shelley explained with a dramatic flair.

"While we British prefer not to discuss things

such as feelings," Prime Minister Falcon said in his usual formal manner, "we very much believe in showing our appreciation, which is why the queen invited you both to tea when she returns to Buckingham Palace next week. Unfortunately, Hammett informed me that due to some trouble back home, you are to return in the morning."

Unable to contain herself, Shelley threw her arms up in the air and shouted, "We're missing the queen?! Why, God? Why?"

"Hmm," Jonathan mumbled. "I wonder what happened."

"You mean to say Hammett hasn't told you?" the prime minister asked, carefully lowering his fork and knife to the plate.

"Told me what?"

The prime minister paused and then looked down at his food as he answered, "I think it best you hear the news from someone in your own government."

Jonathan leaned in, his curiosity piqued. "Why?"

"It's about your family."

"My family?" Jonathan repeated.

"Are they dead?" Shelley blurted out.

"Dead!" Jonathan shrieked, his eyes filling with tears.

"No, Jonathan," Prime Minister Falcon said, staring the boy straight in the eye, "your parents are not dead. They have, however, been arrested for treason."

"That's impossible!" Jonathan answered. "You must be mistaken."

"I assure you, young man, I am not."

"But my parents are dog walkers. And not even very good ones. They lose at least two pets a month," Jonathan said.

"While I don't know all the details of the situation," the prime minister said, "isn't it possible that dog walking was simply their cover?"

"This doesn't make any sense!" Jonathan screeched. "My parents are two of the simplest, most foolish people I've ever met! They can't be spies!"

"Why not?" the prime minister responded. "Look at you."

About the Author

Gitty Daneshvari was an average child, the kind who never made much of a mark academically, athletically, or socially, so it hardly came as a surprise when she was rejected from her school's Talented and Gifted Program. On the contrary, Gitty had long ago accepted that she simply wasn't "special," unless of course you counted her long list of phobias (please read *School of Fear* for further explanation).

Luckily, as Gitty aged, she realized that while she lacked natural talent, there was nothing stopping her from figuring out what she enjoyed and then working hard to become better at it.

Gitty is the author of the series *The League of Unexceptional Children*, *School of Fear*, and *Monster High: Ghoulfriends*. She invites you to visit her online at GittyDaneshvari.com and @GittyDaneshvari.